DATE DUE

SEP 15 2010			
120710			
1-20-10			
JAN 12 2012			
GAYLORD			PRINTED IN U.S.A.

SILENT WITNESS

SILENT WITNESS

•

Nicola Beaumont

AVALON BOOKS
NEW YORK

Published by Thomas Bouregy & Co., Inc.
160 Madison Avenue, New York, NY 10016

Library of Congress Cataloging-in-Publication Data

Beaumont, Nicola.
  Silent witness / Nicola Beaumont.
      p. cm.
  ISBN 978-0-8034-7778-0
  1. Murder—Investigation—Fiction.   I. Title.
  PS3602.E2636S55 2010
  813'.6—dc22
                                        2010006232

PRINTED IN THE UNITED STATES OF AMERICA
ON ACID-FREE PAPER
BY HADDON CRAFTSMEN, BLOOMSBURG, PENNSYLVANIA

To J. C., my heart.
Everything I have and am is yours.

Prologue

The screech of brakes split the silence just before the Buick smashed through the guardrail and tumbled down the steep embankment. Uprooted shrubs and wildflowers hurtled through the air, bouncing off the jagged rock face. Inside the mass of twisting steel, a child's screams echoed through her father's head.

An eternity passed with nothing but the deafening creak of folding metal filling his ears before the car finally rested on its side and all went quiet and still. Distraught, he wrestled with his seat belt, getting his daughter to safety the only thing on his mind. The Buick began to teeter. He stopped cold, even held his breath, waiting for the car to rest.

With slow, deliberate movements, he freed himself from the passenger seat. Once again, the car began to sway. The crack of shattering rocks broke through the silence, and the car slipped to one side, then stilled once again. He resumed his agonizing journey to where his daughter lay unconscious in the back seat.

As he moved, a fierce pain shot through his leg, and he

looked down to see his left thighbone protruding through ripped and bleeding skin. He closed his eyes to the sight, ignoring the pain. He was tough; he could handle it. Vietnam had shown him worse sights than this. His mind reeled with the memory of a small Vietnamese child lying dead across his mother's blood-bathed body. What the damage mortar could do was unbelievable.

His mind darted back to his own child. He tore the already-ripped sleeve from his shirt and used it as a tourniquet around his leg.

Gritting his teeth and ignoring the pain, he inched closer to his daughter.

"Nina?" he whispered, almost afraid to say the name for fear of not getting a response. "Nina, honey. It's Daddy. Can you hear me?"

As he tried to move closer, close enough to check her heartbeat, the jagged bone ripped a little more of his aching flesh, and he succumbed to the searing pain, groaned in agony, then collapsed.

Fifteen years later
Hampton, Virginia

H. Anderson clutched the manila envelope to his chest. Sweat streamed down his face as he dashed across the street. His faded cotton T-shirt reeked with body odor and clung to his aching frame.

He zipped his attention from side to side, his neck swiveling in quick, jerky movements as he checked over his shoulder and down the road. Was anyone watching? Man, he hoped he'd make it. He had to set the record straight, get some sense of redemption after all these years.

A car horn blared. Brakes squealed. Anderson's attention swiveled to the champagne Crown Victoria as it halted only inches from his abdomen. His hand instinctively jammed into the hood. He rolled away, almost losing the manila envelope.

He noticed the driver of the Crown Vic mouth something, but Anderson didn't comprehend. He regained his grip on the package, darted between a few more vehicles, and eyed the mailbox across the road.

Panting, he reached the blue box and dropped the envelope into the slot. For a moment, he breathed a sigh of relief. But only for a moment. Once again, he scanned the street for witnesses.

Adrenaline continued its marathon through his veins as he sprinted back down the street and then entered a tiny upstairs apartment. Plaster fell from the ceiling as he slammed the door. His gaze darted around the room, but he focused on nothing. Nobody would come in here, he told himself. Not that it mattered now. He'd mailed the envelope. The girl would know the truth. He could rest in peace.

He raked the moisture from his brow with the back of his hand and took a deep breath. Crossing the dingy green carpet, he stood next to the bed for endless seconds, his eyes unable to focus, but his mind concentrated on vivid visions from the past. He shivered. God would never forgive him for what he'd done. There really wasn't any point in even asking.

With shaking hands and sweaty palms, he opened the drawer to the bedside table and pulled out a Glock pistol. For several long moments, he eyed the gun as it lay motionless in his hand. He began to cry as he sat on the edge of the bed.

No longer would he feel guilty. No longer would he feel pain.

The gun barrel felt cold to his warm tongue as he gently squeezed the trigger.

Chapter One

Colorado

Nina Thomas glanced at the envelope on the floorboard of her convertible and wondered about the stranger who had sent it. Why come forward after so many years? She had tried to find the mysterious H. Anderson—had gone through the six H. Andersons listed in the Hampton, Virginia, area where the letter had been postmarked, but she'd had no luck. Three had never heard of Shadow Creek, two had hung up on her, and one, she discovered, had committed suicide just two weeks before, leaving his very angry landlady with a considerable bill for back rent and utilities—and according to said landlady— "an apartment she wouldn't be able to ever rent again."

It was then that Nina knew she would have to make the trip to Shadow Creek.

The tree-lined street came to an end as she eased the small two-seater onto the highway. *No turning back now*, she thought, as the white clapboard houses with pro-panel roofs faded into the distance.

Wind whistled across the open top as she pressed on the accelerator. Her cropped hair bounced around her head, tickling the back of her neck, and her stomach rolled on a queasy wave of emotion. She wanted to investigate so badly—needed to investigate—but somehow she knew if she unlocked secrets from the past, things would never be the same again. *She* would never be the same again.

A part of her dreaded that.

The uncertainty of disrupting her life hung in the air around her, picking at her relentlessly. Like the steady drip of a faulty tap. Every time she convinced herself that she needed to know the truth, something—fear, maybe—had her gut stalling, questioning, wondering. Her father was dead. Nothing could change that—even a letter popping up years later that turned an accident into murder.

But what about justice? What about truth? What about? . . .

What about peace, moving on with life, not dwelling on the past? Searching for the truth wouldn't bring him back. It would probably serve no other purpose than to cause her further pain. And her life was finally painless. She'd saved enough money for college, she had a mother and stepfather who loved her more than life, and the dreams were finally beginning to subside.

After all these years, she could finally trust people, she no longer feared going to sleep, no longer had to force herself to touch her head to a pillow. Did she really want to dredge up the past and risk reviving the nightmare that had haunted her entire childhood?

Nina shivered and pressed the button to refit the soft top. At seventy miles an hour, even a July wind could be cold. Deep down, though, Nina knew the chill that hammered her body didn't have anything to do with the wind.

The eerie images still frightened her. Reflections of an unknown creature with the face of a boar and the body of a man—long arms and legs with huge, round black eyes and a stubbed snout. She had never been able to correlate the nightmare to the crash, but within the depths of her soul, she knew the two were related.

Struggle as she might, she still couldn't remember the accident, except for a vague image of her daddy and a big green helicopter. The psychologists she had been shuffled to as a child told her the memories might come into focus one day, but not to pin her hopes on it. She had been awfully young, they'd said, and might never regain the memory of that one traumatic incident.

Instead of realistic memories, an eight-year-old Nina had created her own version of what had happened that day. She was convinced the helicopter had been her father's vehicle to heaven, and as much as her mother had tried to persuade her there was no helicopter involved, Nina had still believed.

Then, one night when she was twelve, she dreamed of another man being in the car with them. The person—just the misty haze of a faceless man in a blue suit—had helped her father into the Heaven Helicopter and taken him into the sky. The thought that the blue-suited man was an angel stayed with her until she was old enough to rationalize that angels don't wear blue suits, and God doesn't need a helicopter.

Her mind came back to the present, and she nodded to a trucker passing her in a metallic, lavender-flecked Peterbilt before turning her attention to the radio. Static hissed through the speakers, so she flipped to the AM band.

"Just remember, my faithful brothers and sisters, that our God is not a God of fear, but of peace. Walk with the Lord in righteousness, and you shall find peace." As the preacher's voice drew out the "s"-sound in peace, Nina forgot the road and stared down at the radio as if the voice had spoken to her directly.

She wasn't a religious person, but recently, she had started to realize that she'd lived a great deal of her life in fear. Fear that people would think she was crazy for having to see a shrink. Fear that she should remember and couldn't. Fear that she would never save enough money for college.

Funny thing was, fear was even driving her right now. Fear that if she ignored the letter H. Anderson had sent, she'd regret it for the rest of her life. Fear that if she investigated, she would find nothing but trouble . . . Fear that she'd discover her father wasn't the honorable man she'd always believed he was.

Ironic that the preacher would touch on that right now, this minute.

She glanced at the asphalt shoulder as another mile marker ticked by. In another eight hours, she would be driving the same stretch of road that had claimed her father's life and changed hers forever. Was this trip such a good idea after all? She still wasn't sure.

She clicked off the radio, not wanting any more advice. She'd committed to this. She wasn't a quitter. She'd see it through, even if it killed her.

She hoped it didn't kill her.

Shadow Creek, Arizona, situated near Flagstaff, lay surrounded by stately pines. Miles off the highway, the small suburb rarely received visitors. Only once had there been some excitement. That was when some crazy war vet had plunged down a cliff, killed himself, and almost taken his daughter with him. That's how the story went, anyway. Few people were left in Shadow Creek who had been around at the time. The failing copper mines had driven many people away over the intervening years. Now, any truth to the various stories that made their rounds through the small community was difficult to decipher. Rylan Andies—his present identity, anyway—had spent the past few years listening to the rabble, and he thought he'd finally figured out the truth.

Today he sat perched behind a fallen pine in the middle of

the tree-filled divided roadway in an Arizona Highway Patrol car. The little red convertible zipped by him, the petite blond driver paying him no attention whatsoever. He watched with deliberate intent as she eased into the fast lane to allow another car to merge onto the freeway. His laser told him she wasn't speeding, so he knew she'd be surprised when he pulled her over.

Ry flipped on his lights and siren and flew out onto I-40. As he closed the distance between them, he could see the alarm in her eyes as she checked her rearview mirror. He felt like a jerk for scaring her this way, but he had to find out what she was up to. Surveillance had told him she was headed toward Arizona, but that didn't mean she was actually going to Shadow Creek.

Not that he thought she wasn't. Shadow Creek was the only place she could be going. She hadn't stepped two feet outside her hometown in years, and then two weeks after his father kills himself, she's on her way down memory lane. That wasn't a coincidence. He didn't know what the connection was, but he knew there was one.

He eyed the tail light Pritchard had popped when she'd stopped for gas a couple of hours ago, and then watched as she dutifully slowed her vehicle and parked it on the graveled shoulder.

His tires bit into the pebbly ground as he eased the patrol car to a stop behind her. Ry paused behind the steering wheel, hating himself and his job. He knew he needed to protect her, but the lies and deception that were an integral part of his job were starting to get on his nerves. She didn't deserve this— not this scare from him, and definitely not the mess she was walking into.

He let out an oath and pushed open the patrol car door. He could see her shuffling around inside her vehicle, probably looking for her driver's license. The thought that he was a heel grew roots and made a home inside his mind.

As he stepped up to her door, she rolled down the window and peered up at him with wide chestnut eyes that radiated apprehension.

It's your job, man. Just do it and get it over with.

Her gaze darted between his face, the metal badge pinned to his tan uniform, and his G.I. pistol holstered at his hip.

"Officer, I wasn't speeding was I?" She brought her gaze back to his. She was looking at him as if he were death looming over.

He hoped he wasn't.

"Ma'am, your driver's license, registration, and insurance please."

"But Officer—"

"License, registration, and insurance."

She rifled through her purse again, then clicked open the glove compartment for her registration and proof of insurance. When she turned back to hand him the information, her gaze slammed into his chest like a bullet. Confusion etched her features—and fear. Not a fear of getting a ticket, but more a fear of the unknown—that doe-in-the-headlights look he'd witnessed so many times over the years. He really didn't like himself right now. This was a cruel game, but one that had to be played to the full if he were going to glean from her the information he needed.

"Please, Officer, tell me what this is all about. I wasn't speeding, was I?" Ry raked over the documents without a look or a word to her. He knew if he looked into those beautiful eyes of hers, he'd lose it.

"Everything seems to be in order, ma'am." He handed Nina her belongings. "May I ask where you're headed?" He glanced down the highway avoiding her eyes for the moment, while he silently chided himself for losing his cool. He didn't understand why this whole thing had gotten to him. He only knew it had. Chestnut—no, *brown*—eyes shouldn't have an affect on him. Three years undercover had fried his brain.

"Sh-shadow Creek. Why?"

Ry wrote out the warning, and then turned back to her, putting on an Academy Award-winning smile. The one he knew always worked. He tipped his hat then handed Nina the slip of paper. "Just a warning, ma'am. You have a tail light out. There's a place in Shadow Creek that can fix you right up."

She glanced backward. "Tail light?"

"Yes, ma'am. This is just a warning, but you need to get that fixed as soon as possible."

Nina stared at the slip. "Of course."

She set her gaze on him, and he tipped his hat. Her doe-eyed gaze softened, and the urge to run his hand down her smooth cheek hit him hard. Quickly, he looked away from her face, his focus landing on the petite hands perched on the edge of the open window. Long sleek fingers tipped with pearly white polished nails filled his vision. Slowly, he raked his gaze up her arm and to the hollow of her neck. Her pulse jumped out at him in rhythm, and he blinked hard, mentally cajoling himself to stay focused.

Oh, man, he was in trouble.

"Well, thank you, Officer. Am I free to go now?" His attention was riveted to her face once again, and he swallowed the sensual stupidity that loomed over him like a guillotine.

"Yes, ma'am. Have a good day." He made his way back to his car and watched as she checked her mirror then eased onto the interstate. He didn't need the radar to know she kept her speed under the limit.

When she was out of sight, Harry R. Anderson, Jr., alias Richard Moore, alias Harold Greenwood, alias Ry Andies, or any number of other names, depending on his current job description, got into the patrol car. He pulled off the blond hairpiece that he had used as a disguise, and tossed it onto the seat next to him. He vigorously scratched his sweating head of black hair—That blasted wig always made his head sweat. He picked up the microphone. "Eagle to Nest."

"Go ahead, this is Nest," the speaker replied.

"She's on I-40. Should reach Shadow Creek about nineteen hundred hours."

"You kept your cover, right?"

Ry sighed into the mouthpiece, not even trying to hide his disgust. "What do you take me for? I'm not a rookie. Besides, I wore that stupid wig. My own mother wouldn't have recognized me. What more do you want?"

"Keep me informed of every move she makes. We can't let her get too close."

"I will," Anderson assured his boss. "Over and out."

He replaced the microphone as his thoughts returned to Nina Thomas. After reading the lengthy file on her, he really felt as if he knew her. Beautiful. Intelligent. Loyal. Too bad she'd decided to snoop. He hated to see her get hurt after staying out of it for so many years.

What a waste.

But what troubled him more than anything was his own reaction to her. He'd had to keep reminding himself she was just another assignment. She needed to be protected, but so did he. He'd spent too long living with his secrets to allow anyone to ruin everything now. He had to find a way to complete his assignment *and* keep her safe. He wasn't sure yet how he was going to accomplish it, but he knew he would.

One thing he did know for sure. Daydreaming about her was only going to get them both killed.

Chapter Two

The evening sun drooped, splaying shards of lavender and orange across the unmarred sky. The rich scent of pine breezed in through the vents of Nina's car, and she filled her nostrils with the heady aroma as she gazed in appreciation at the thick forest edging the highway. Northern Arizona was as beautiful to behold as her hometown nestled within the Colorado Rockies. She hoped being here would help her remember the time she'd had with her father before he died.

She flipped on her turn indicator and eased the car down the off ramp. As she turned the corner, the sun blazed its glory below the car's visor, and she squinted, using her left hand as a shield. She'd have to wait until tomorrow to begin her investigation. She wouldn't be able to see much of the road in the growing twilight.

She downshifted into fourth as she hit the Shadow Creek town limits and eyed the street for any restaurant that didn't look like cockroaches had taken over.

The two-lane road wended its way between small shops decorated with quaint, striped awnings. Many of the businesses were restaurants, but all were closed and seemed dismally silent in the copper haze formed by the setting sun.

Passing the bed-and-breakfast where she had made a reservation, Nina continued to look for a place to eat. Almost at the end of Main Street, she noticed an open drive-in restaurant. A confetti of cars sprinkled the parking lot, and a street lamp illuminated the front entrance. A gauche neon sign atop the roof blinked "Mac's Drive-up." Nina shrugged. It didn't look gourmet, but it was open, and it was food.

She slipped the car into first gear and eased into a parking spot. With a cursory glance at the menu, she pushed the order button. The speaker crackled to life. "Welcome to Mac's. May I take your order?"

"Cheeseburger, fries, and a Coke, please," Nina replied, ignoring the fact that lately she'd gained a few pounds and should have probably opted for a salad and a bottle of spring water.

Sitting at Mac's Drive-up, eating the rock patty they called a hamburger, Nina sifted through some of the paperwork she had brought with her—copies of her father's birth and death certificates, newspaper clippings her mother had kept, and a barrage of other things she thought might be important the day she'd packed, but which now looked useless.

Working at the library hadn't really been as helpful as she would have expected when she began her investigation. The small Colorado branch where she clerked didn't house any information about out-of-state, small-town incidences, and although she could have requisitioned them, once she had learned of H. Anderson's suicide, she'd known she had to come to Shadow Creek. Even though the thought of dredging up the past frightened her, if this H. Anderson had risked his life to make sure she discovered that her father had been murdered, then she felt obligated to find out what had really happened.

She sipped soda from a straw and closed her eyes, willing

herself to remember the past. It remained a mystery to her why anyone would kill her father. If he had been someone who deserved to die, wouldn't she remember something horrible about him?

And what about her? For the first time, she wondered if she was to have been killed also. As the question entered her mind, an unyielding doubt slinked into her soul. Instinctively, she glanced around at the almost-deserted Main Street and the sprinkling of cars that patronized Mac's Drive-up. Was coming to Shadow Creek such a good idea after all?

She swallowed a bite of hamburger seasoned with dread and said a silent prayer for her safety.

Chapter Three

Washington, D.C.

Lance Edward Lottawalski, or Sir Lancelot as his buddies called him, sat at his large mahogany desk, rubbing a handkerchief across the top of his balding head. The perspiration, he tried to convince himself, was caused by the July humidity. Never would he admit that some twenty-three-year-old kid could make him nervous.

Regardless of whether he would admit it, though, Nina Thomas *was* making him nervous. Why couldn't she have just left well enough alone? She had a good life. She had always had a good life; he'd helped see to that. Why, after all these years had she decided to make a nuisance of herself? It didn't make sense.

He stuffed the handkerchief into the breast pocket of his navy suit, picked up the nearest pen and began scribbling on a sticky note. The pen was out of ink.

"I don't need this right now." He growled and slammed the ballpoint into the trashcan beside his desk, then searched for another pen. "I've got to deal with Harry blowing his brains out, and if Carlucci gets wind of . . ." He let his aggravated mumbling die off as he scribbled a note and then shoved it into the same pocket with his sweat-soaked hanky.

The wheels of his chair rolled easily across the hard plastic carpet-saver stretching out from under his desk as he unceremoniously pushed himself away. He grabbed his briefcase and sprinted out the door.

"Out to lunch, Sue," he said as he flashed by his secretary.

"What do you mean she's in Shadow Creek snooping around?" Anthony Carlucci pounded the ground with his expensive Italian imports as he paced in front of Ry. "I thought she didn't know anything." He turned a fierce eye toward Ry.

Ry played the part of the intimidated minion well. After three years, he had it down to a science. He made eye contact with Carlucci only tentatively then shoved his hands into the pockets of his cotton twill pants.

The air in the tiny warehouse office tasted gritty as he dragged in a slow breath. He exhaled and took his next breath through his nostrils. The Texas humidity became a part of him as he watched Carlucci kick a dust bunny under the plain metal desk.

The man turned to face Ry again, and it took all of his trained ability to keep his mouth shut. He couldn't stand the chump who stood before him, but he also knew that now was not the time to offer advice. Carlucci was livid, his olive complexion ringed in white wherever the adrenaline pumped a voracious line through his body.

"I thought she was just another poor little victim. Nothing to worry about. A harmless kid. Now you tell me she's in Shadow Creek? What am I doing listening to you bozos? I should've eliminated her when I first found out she was still alive."

He shoved one lean hand into his pants pocket and, with the other hand, ran fingers through the graying temple of his thick black hair.

"But, boss—"

"Don't 'but boss' me. I'm sick of your good-for-nothing excuses, Andies, now get back out to that town and make sure you're right about her. If it looks like she knows something—*anything*—I don't care how trivial it may seem to your pea-brained mind, take care of it. Do you understand?"

"Yes, boss. And don't worry. She doesn't know anything. She was just a kid. Don't panic, Mr. Carlucci. If she knew something, she would have gone to the Feds ages ago."

Carlucci threw Ry a look that let the him know just what he thought of that idea. "And I suppose you forgot about that double-crossing DEA jerk?" Carlucci sucked in a deep breath that made his chest puff out like a posed rooster.

Ry dropped his gaze to the dusty floor below his feet.

"Look, I know we don't need to risk taking someone out right now. Not with the biggest deal of our lives about to go down, but I'm telling you good, Andies, you keep an eye on her. She gets too close, and I'm not taking any chances."

Ry met Carlucci's gaze. The criminal stared back with steely conviction. "You keep a good eye on her, Andies, or you'll be going right down with her, got it?"

"Yes, sir. Loud and clear."

Ry left the warehouse and found his way to the small apartment Carlucci let him keep in Texas. Things were not going as smoothly as he had planned. In fact, things were not going smoothly at all. The girl was causing too much of a ruckus. He'd hoped Carlucci wouldn't find out about her—but then, he should have known better than that. Carlucci owned Shadow Creek; there wasn't a person in the whole town who could be trusted.

Ry grabbed a suitcase off the top shelf in the closet and began stuffing it with clothes. One more trip to Shadow Creek. He had originally anticipated being out of this whole situation by next week, but now both sides were up in arms, and he was stuck swinging in the wind, waiting for things to die down.

What was she doing anyway—besides making his life a living hell? He'd already been flying here and there so often he had invented a new disease called Chronic Jetlag Syndrome. How he'd been able to keep everything under wraps this long was a mystery even to him. Now, things were really getting dodgy, and he was on his way back to hell on earth, in the middle of nowhere, and had to tail a person, incognito, in a town with the population of The Garden of Eden—*plus* hold his cover.

It wouldn't work, he decided as he slammed down the suitcase lid and secured the latch. Someone would find him out, and he'd end up in a pine box six feet deep—all for the protection of some chick who should've just kept her nose out of it.

She sure had a cute nose, though. And her lush lips, almost pouting, had . . . Ry mentally shook himself. He couldn't afford to think of her as a woman, he had to think of her merely as an assignment.

Still, having to keep close tabs on her wasn't the most horrible job he'd ever had. He picked up the suitcase and headed out the door. Maybe by some miracle everything would work out before someone ended up dead. He could hope, at least.

According to the brochure, the Lamplighter Bed & Breakfast, one of three motels in Shadow Creek, consisted of a strip of twelve cabin-like rooms, a separate main lobby with a dining room and kitchen, and a cabin in which the owners, Margaret and Harvey Orwell, resided. It wasn't much to look at, Nina decided as she'd parked her car in front of the door marked OFFICE. Dust swirled up to greet her as her boots disturbed the gravelly ground. She swiped her hand across her nose, killing the urge to sneeze.

It didn't really matter that the place looked as if it had stood since the beginning of time, she decided, as long as it was clean.

Her doubts about the place were put to rest when she finally met Margaret and Harvey. They were a nice, friendly, fiftyish couple, both round and polyester, and they welcomed Nina as if she were family.

"Why, you darlin' soul, you didn't have to stop over at that awful Mac's Drive-up. I would have gladly fixed you a bowl of soup if you'd come straight here," Margaret Orwell gazed at Nina with sympathetic, aged blue eyes.

"It wasn't all that bad." Nina wished she had come straight here, though. The rich aroma of beef stew blanketed the foyer in a homey atmosphere that Nina had thought only existed in movies. Even her mother wasn't that great at cooking. Which was probably why she'd never really taken to it either. "I've had worse, actually, and it's usually come from my own kitchen."

Harvey Orwell's deep guffaw echoed through the lobby and bounced off the dark brown paneling. Nina glanced at Margaret, and they both laughed.

"You won't find no frozen food 'round this place," Harvey said, patting Margaret on the shoulder. "This little filly here's an excellent cook. Dern good at most ever'thing she does."

"Aw, Harv, you're embarrassing me in front of our guest. Why don't you get out from behind this counter and take her suitcase to her room for her? That is your job, you know." Margaret's playful chiding and the obviously rehearsed look of hurt that Harvey returned his wife eased Nina's mind for the first time since she'd received the letter from H. Anderson.

She had been wrought with guilt over not telling her mother the truth about this trip, but she'd known that Emma Thomas would've canceled her second honeymoon. Watching the Orwells enjoy each other like this gave Nina the peace of mind she needed right now. She may have kept her mother and stepfather in the dark a little, but at least she knew they were enjoying each other rather than sitting at home worrying about her. They didn't need that kind of stress.

And, frankly, neither did she.

"All right, Mags, don't get your britches in a bundle." Harvey rounded the counter and picked up Nina's tiny suitcase. "C'mon, sweets. I'll show to your room. A young girl like you could get lost all alone in a big hotel like this." He grinned and held his arm crooked for Nina to use as a guide.

Nina curved the corners of her mouth, slipped her hand through his proffered arm, and let him lead the way. At the door, she looked back over her shoulder to Margaret. "See you in the morning. I think I'm going to like it here."

"So what brings a young thing like you to a beat-up old town like this anyhow?" Harvey asked as they crossed the gravel lot to the strip of rooms.

"Just doing a bit of research." Nina took in the evening air. A spattering of stars dotted the subdued sky. Cicadas sang from their hiding places beneath the shrubbery and pines that formed the canvas for the sleepy town of Shadow Creek. But that needle of dread still pricked the back of her mind, and she wasn't sure she should tell anyone the reason for her trip.

"You in college or something'?"

"Nothing like that. Just a personal interest in a story I heard." Nina stalled, and then decided she couldn't be too secretive about why she was in Shadow Creek. If she didn't ask questions, she'd never find out the reason her father was killed. Besides, she'd been a child when it had happened, and she didn't have an enemy in the world and had never done anything to hurt anyone in her entire life. She was safe. This silly apprehension was just that—silly.

"Don't suppose you remember a car accident that happened about fifteen years ago, do you?"

"You must be talking about that crazy Vietnam vet that crashed off over the side of Old Shadow Creek Highway," Harvey replied. "Yeah, I remember it. Me and Mags had just moved here from Texas 'round about that time, if'n I recall correctly." Harvey shrugged, and then, as they approached the room, reached for the door key. "Why you interested in that old story?"

"Just curious. You know anything about it?"

"Well, I remember the guy. He was nice enough while he was livin' here. Kept to hisself pretty much, but wasn't unfriendly when you passed him in the street." Harvey opened the door and waited for Nina to go in first. "They lived here, just the two of them, him and his little girl, for—oh, I'd say about a year," he continued. "I heard rumors that him and his wife had split up, but I don't rightly know the truth of it. We was all surprised when he plunged hisself over the edge like that, especially since he had his youngen with him. If you didn't know anything else about old Pete, you knew he loved that girl. You could see it in his eyes ever' time he looked at her." Harvey put down the suitcase and went over to the bedside table to drop the room key.

"Anyhow, he packed all their things one day and, without a word, threw hisself over the edge. Rumors were, it had something to do with drugs and cops, but I don't know. He seemed like a nice enough fella to me."

He turned to face her. "You okay?" Harvey crossed the room to her. "You look a little peaked."

Nina propped herself against the doorjamb, unable to support herself. She felt as if someone had just punched her in the throat. Drugs? Cops? *Suicide?* Something inside her pleaded for her to forget this plight and go home—just let her present memories remain undisturbed. But another part of her knew she couldn't do that.

She dragged in a deep breath and let it out slowly. "I—I'm fine. I just got a little dizzy for a minute, that's all. I'll be all right."

"If you're sure, I'll leave you be, but if you need anything—anything at all—don't you hesitate to give me or the missus a call, you hear? We don't want none of our guests ailin'." Harvey briefly put a comforting arm around her shoulder. "I'll tell you what. I'm gonna go and have Mags bring you a nice hot cup of cocoa. You've had a long drive comin' all the way from Colorada. You're plum exhausted."

The digital clock read 10:05 when Nina awoke the next morning. She'd missed breakfast. She couldn't believe she had slept so late. It wasn't like her. She propped herself up on one elbow and pulled the covers to her chin. Looking around the room, she realized she didn't even remember undressing for bed. She took note of the faded plaid loveseat and oak table lamp set diagonally in the opposite corner from the bed. The red, green, and black checks matched the bed quilt and curtains. She shook her head slowly. How could she have been so oblivious? She remembered Harvey and Margaret Orwell— she smiled at the thought of them. Remembered Harvey leaving, but that was all. She couldn't think of a time when she'd been so thoroughly knocked out.

She frowned at her open suitcase on the floor, all the belongings strewn sloppily about. She must have been beyond tired to be that messy. She swung her feet onto the floor and curled her toes around the plush forest green carpet. It was time to get her investigation started, so she needed to get to the library and the police station.

She stretched a bit and then got out of bed. Her brain felt thick and the room spun. She grabbed the bedside table to steady herself. What had happened last night?

Regaining her balance, she shuffled to the shower.

The warm water eased Nina's tense muscles as she let the shower rain over her.

Rich Willis sat at the round Formica-topped table reading the front page of the *Denver Post*. It was a lousy morning. The coffee pot had overflowed, and the Virginia humidity was already making his bare legs stick to the flowered plastic chair. He folded the paper and picked up the spoon that had fallen into his cereal bowl. Nothing of interest happened in Colorado anymore. Why he still read that paper, he didn't know. Just some habit he could never seem to break, he supposed.

With mouth ready, Rich was about to eat a spoonful of corn flakes when the phone rang and startled him. He bit out an oath as he dropped the spoon back into the cereal bowl.

He picked up a napkin and wiped splashed milk from his hairy arms before racing across the room to silence the annoying ring. "Yeah?"

"Where have you been all night?" Rich recognized Lottawalski's voice through the static from his cellular.

"Oh, it's you. I haven't been anywhere. Why?"

"We've got major problems. I've been trying to reach you since yesterday, noon. You haven't been answering your phone."

"Well, I was trying to get some info about Carlucci. For some reason I had a sneaking suspicion that he was onto me."

"Anderson's got him under control, don't worry, but I need to see you right away. You're not going to believe what happened."

"Well, don't beat around the bush."

"I can't talk about it over the phone. I'll be there in fifteen minutes."

"I'll be here." Rich replaced the receiver and went back to his half-eaten bowl of cereal.

The flakes were soggy. Rich sighed, took the bowl to the sink and washed the mush down the garbage disposal. So much for breakfast again today. Rich's morning meals had been disrupted ever since Harry Anderson killed himself. Harry's death had brought a frightening sense of finality that seemed to extend to Rich. Then, the nightmare developed— Nina lying on top of her father's dead body. It was the first time in fifteen years he'd seen Pete's face. Nina, still a child, looking so forlorn, crying uncontrollably as blood pooled around her father's corpse. The terrifying image had Rich's sleep-deprived body using each morning to track Carlucci's every movement.

Anderson or no Anderson, Rich needed to know the facts.

He opened the refrigerator, grabbed a drink-box of orange juice and made his way into the small front room. He plopped down on the dirt-brown hide-a-bed and looked around the room, not really seeing anything. He'd never been good at waiting, and his stomach knotted into tiny bows of uneasiness as time slowly ticked by while he waited for Lottawalski.

He got up and began to pace the small strip of carpet between the couch and the beat-up old coffee table, unable to sit still. "I haven't blown it, have I?" he asked himself for the umpteenth time since Harry's suicide. Man, if Carlucci knew the truth . . . but he couldn't, Rich reminded himself. "Pete's long gone," he mumbled.

He chugged the orange juice from the hole he'd cut in the side of the carton, then crushed the box and tossed it across the room. He studied his watch. It had been ten minutes since the call from Lance. Felt more like a lifetime. If the guy didn't show up pronto, Rich was going to ring his neck.

Nina wrestled on a pair of Wrangler jeans and pulled her Ropers onto her feet. The shower had woken her up a bit, but she still felt a little groggy and couldn't remember much about the previous evening. Her head throbbed so badly she didn't even want to remember.

Deciding to see if she could squeeze some breakfast out of Margaret Orwell, she grabbed her door key and headed across the gravel parking lot.

When Nina entered the lobby, Margaret was on the phone. She smiled and waved Nina in. Putting her hand over the mouthpiece of the receiver, Margaret whispered, "I'm on hold. I hate that, don't you?"

Nina nodded and sat down to wait in one of the plastic green chairs.

"Yes, dang it, of course I understand."

Nina, surprised by the older woman's hostile outburst didn't want to appear nosy, so she picked up an ancient issue of *Sports Illustrated* and started browsing through the pages. As she reached the last page, Margaret hung up the phone and leaned on the counter.

"Good mornin', princess. Did you sleep okay?" Her accent dripped sweetness and Nina wondered if she'd imagined the woman's biting tone on the telephone. Her head *was* still a little fuzzy.

"Fine." Nina put down the magazine and walked over to the counter. "Actually, I slept too well. I don't even remember getting ready for bed, and I'm usually up at dawn. You sure must provide a comfy bed."

"Well, t'tell you the truth, Ol' Harv told me you was feeling kind of ill, so I went over with some hot chocolate. I guess it knocked you out pretty good." Margaret fidgeted with some papers on the counter and shuffled them into a neat pile.

"Why would hot chocolate do that?" Nina asked.

"Well, you looked pretty bushed, so I put a little sleepin' aid in it for you. Hope you don't mind. I was just trying to help."

"Can't say as I would've approved last night, Mrs. Orwell, but this morning I seem to be fine."

"You best call me Mags. Ever'body else does. And let's get you some nice hot biscuits and gravy. Got some keeping warm in the kitchen." She waved at the archway to her left. "Go on in the dining room and find yerself a seat."

Rich practically yanked off the doorknob when the bell rang. Lottawalski stood on the other side smiling.

"You've been pacing the floor ever since I called, I take it?" he asked.

"Funny, Lance, very funny." Rich stepped aside. "You could've told me something on the phone instead of making me sweat, you know. Even if it had just been that I had nothing to worry about."

"I like to see you sweat, Willis. Don't you know that?"

Rich didn't appreciate Lottawalski's sarcasm, but he let the man into his apartment anyway. "Just give me the scoop."

"Okay, okay." Lottawalski crossed the room and sank into the ragged sofa. "But you're not going to like it. Sit down." He nodded to the torn leather recliner opposite the couch and then glanced at the empty orange juice box on the floor. "You live like a pig, Rich. No wonder your wife left you."

Rich didn't respond to Lottawalski's goad. It was an old rib between them, and he didn't feel like playing right now. He glanced at the recliner and decided not to sit. He was too antsy for anything as inert as sitting. He put his attention on his friend. "So?"

Lottawalski sighed. "It's Nina."

"What?" Rich slumped into the recliner. "What about her?"

"She's in Shadow Creek."

Rich raked his hands over the top of his head. He sat forward and looked into Lottawalski's face. "What's she doing there?"

"I don't know yet. But I hope Anderson's hunch about his father isn't the reason. If Harry contacted her before he died, and she starts snooping around, she could blow the entire operation. All these years of hard work, down the tubes."

"What do you want me to do?"

"Nothing."

"I can't do 'nothing'. Her life may be in danger." Rich got up and went to the window, peering out at nothing in particular.

"I can't believe this is happening." He shook his head and turned back to Lance. "I can't believe this is happening," he repeated, as if saying it again might bring about belief.

"She's safe. Anderson's keeping an eye on her, and Carlucci doesn't know anything anyway. All he knows is that she's there. Anderson had to tell him that much, but he thinks she's there for no reason in particular. We told the press that Harry didn't leave a note, so I'm sure Carlucci thinks the secrets died with him."

Rich's mind remained uneasy. The girl was young and oblivious to the danger she might be walking into. It would be too easy for her to become another murder statistic. He didn't think he could handle it if that happened. "I don't know, Lance. Do you think Anderson can handle it on his own?"

"Don't worry."

"But . . ."

"Don't even think about it, Rich, they're two different people. Look, you're my friend; that's why I wanted to tell you about it myself and in person, but don't do anything stupid. Let us professionals handle it, okay?" Lottawalski met Rich at the window. "You can't do anything. Understand me. You can't."

Lance started for the door. "Don't worry. Everything is under control."

"It better be, Lancelot. It better be."

"You won't be seeing me for a while. I'm going to lay low and discreet. I suggest you do the same. Anderson will keep us informed. If he needs any help, we'll be the first to know. Let him take care of it."

"But . . ." Rich turned from the window and started to follow his friend.

Lottawalski held up his hand, silencing Rich's protest. "Let him take care of it. If you try to interfere, you might end up

blowing his cover and the whole operation at the same time—
not to mention the fact that you'd stand a good chance of getting everyone killed, including Nina. So just stay out of it."

"All right," Rich conceded. He pushed Lance out the door.
"Now get going. I have to go to work before my boss fires me.
God forbid I didn't have Construction Warehouse to go to
every day."

Lottawalski turned back to face Rich. He held out his hand.
"Thanks. And have a nice day." He pasted on a smile and
bowed slightly.

Instead of shaking the offered hand, Rich slapped it. "I don't
know why I'm still friends with you, Lancelot. You've always
been a jerk." He rolled his eyes in mock disgust then shut the
door.

As he closed the door, he could just hear the fading sound
of Lance's chuckle. They'd been like brothers since Vietnam,
and Rich knew his friend was only trying to protect everyone
involved. Still, there was no way he was staying put and doing
nothing.

Absolutely no way.

Ry Andies got off the plane and collected his baggage. He
was tired, and all he could think about was getting back to the
rat-hole of an apartment he called home while he resided in
Shadow Creek. After hours on one plane, the puddle-jump
from Phoenix to Flagstaff had been turbulent, and his stomach
needed a good dose of antacid to calm it. He'd have to stop at
the drugstore on the way to Shadow Creek and pick some up.

As he made his way to his trusty steed, a classic 1955 Chevy
Belair, he thought about Nina Thomas. The only way he could
really keep tabs on her was to get close, real close, and stay that
way. It would be pretty tough, though, unless he could think of
a feasible reason to approach her. He'd have to do something
quickly or else he wouldn't have anything to report to Car-

lucci. If that happened, people—people named Nina—would end up dead. Of that, Ry had no doubt.

Getting home, he plopped himself onto the chintzy sofa and put his feet over the arm. His suitcase lay in the middle of the room, where he'd dumped it, and his car keys were sprawled on the glass top of the coffee table. It had sounded like the glass split when he dropped them there, but he was too tired to take a second look.

He tried to kick off his shoes, but the laces were too tight, and he had to pry his head off the sofa to untie them. As one shoe dropped to the floor, his big toe peeped out of a hole in his sock. *Irritating!* After getting off the other shoe, Ry ripped his socks from his feet in disgust then flopped backward.

With his arm across his eyes, he fell asleep and didn't wake up until the phone rang at 1 A.M. It was a wrong number.

"Who are you trying to call at this time of the morning, anyway?" he yelled into the receiver.

"Sorry, man," the voice said before hanging up and leaving Ry with a dial tone buzzing in his ear.

Mad as he was, he took the time to get up and find his way to the bedroom in the hopes that he could go back to sleep until at least nine.

Chapter Four

Nina ate her breakfast slowly, leaving half of it unfinished on her plate. It wasn't that the food was unsatisfying. In fact, the food was excellent, but Nina's appetite hadn't woken up yet.

"What's the matter? You don't like my cookin'?" Margaret asked.

"It's not that, Mrs. Orwell. I'm just not very hungry. I appreciate you fixing it for me, though." Nina gave the woman a tiny smile in compensation.

"If you don't start calling me Mags, I'm gonna have to boot you out of here." Margaret wagged her finger at Nina.

"Well, thank you for breakfast, *Mags,*" Nina teased. She scooted her chair back and stood to leave. "And have a nice day, *Mags.*" She laughed now, and backed up toward the door.

Margaret stood defiantly with her hands on her hips. "I don't know 'bout you youngens these days." She shook her head and shooed Nina out the door before clearing the table, but Nina didn't miss the amusement in the older woman's eyes. They sparkled with a girlish mischief that would appeal to everyone.

Still, something about the woman's hostile tone on the telephone niggled in the back of Nina's mind. For now, she let it go. She had other things to discover.

Nina went back across the parking lot and into her room to find the mysterious letter she had received. Maybe if she read it one more time it would all make sense.

Lying prone across the bed, she pulled the scribbled pages from the envelope and began to read:

Nina Thomas,

I am so sorry about your father. I didn't plan on things getting as bad as they eventually did. I am sorry. I hope you can forgive me and understand that I wasn't always a bad person. The Agency was very good to me. I shouldn't have turned my back on them. It's my fault you lost your father. It's my fault you almost lost your life. I thought that Tony could make my life better. He promised so much. I turned my back on everything I believed in. I should've just completed my assignment and not been lured in by the money, the drugs, the tequila. Please forgive me. I wish I could tell you more, but I can't. All you need to know is that I am responsible, and I am sorry. If it's any consolation, I have been paying for my mistakes for the past 15 years. I hope you can find it in your heart to forgive me.

H. Anderson

P.S.: Sorry, Junior. No reflection on you.

Nina read the letter three times before rolling onto her back and sitting up. She still didn't understand how this man, H. Anderson, was responsible for her father's death. The letter was more like a teaser than an explanation. If this H. Anderson was going to take the time to write, why didn't he take the time to explain? And who was "Junior?" Frustrated, she read the letter again. Still she couldn't make heads or tails of it.

She wadded the note and threw it across the room, and then quickly ran to the corner, where it had landed, to retrieve it. "Good job, Nina," she chided herself aloud. "Mutilate the only lead you have." She ironed the paper with her hand until it was legible again, then folded it neatly and put it in her shoulder bag. She studied the snapshot that had arrived with the letter. Three soldiers stared back at her from the past. One she recognized as her father. The others weren't familiar, although she assumed one of them must be H. Anderson. Putting the three-by-five into the manila envelope and stuffing them under the bed pillow, she decided on a positive course of action. The best place to start would be the library, researching through old newspapers about her father's accident to see if the name H. Anderson was connected in any way.

Ry rolled out of bed at 9:30 A.M., glad his shift at the station didn't start until three. He was still groggy from his bumpy flight and broken sleep. If he could've gotten his hands on the bozo who'd woken him up at 1 A.M., Ry would have strangled him for sure.

Shuffling over to the dresser, he pulled out underwear, socks, and a T-shirt and stumbled to the bathroom. Standing in the shower, he closed his eyes and let the cool water wake him up. The spray was refreshing, and by the time he turned it off, he was fully awake. The only task now was to down a few cups of coffee before really having to start the day.

Sitting at the round, glass-topped dinette table, he sipped on coffee almost strong enough to be espresso and thought about how not to get killed. A lot had to do with Harper. If the sheriff didn't suspect anything, chances were Carlucci wouldn't either. And Harper, being the gullible creeper he was, should be easy enough to control as long as Andies kept his cool. Ry grimaced. Mealy-mouthed Harper had become a constant irritation. Sometimes Ry wished murder was legal, but he had

more important things to plan this morning. He had to figure
out what he was going to do about the girl. How he was going
to get close to her without tipping anybody off—and without
getting her killed. How was he going to? . . . He shook his
head and sighed heavily. "You'll think of something," he said
aloud.

Putting his mug in the dishwasher, he grabbed a pair of
Levi's and a plaid shirt off the back of the chair and finished
getting dressed. Finding his boots was a task, but after a few
dead ends, he found them under the couch. Pulling them on,
he headed out the door.

The Shadow Creek library was small, with only a dozen or
so book shelves. Nina hadn't stepped two feet inside the door
before her hopes evaporated. It was going to be impossible to
find out anything in here.

A rotund, silver-haired lady sat behind a scarred desk. She
gave Nina a cheerful smile. "Hi, my dear. Are you new in
town?"

Nina nodded. "Just visiting. Thought I'd come in and look
at some of the things Shadow Creek has to offer. You know,
learn a bit about the town? Its history, stuff like that." She
looked around the tiny library, trying to look impressed. "This
is a lovely place."

The librarian's lips split into a wide smile. She shrugged.
"It's small, but it suits us." She pushed back her chair, and the
legs screeched across the hardwood floor in protest. "Let me
just show you where we keep the old back issues of newspapers."

She hesitated and searched Nina's face. "The *Chronicle* will
be all right? I'm afraid that's about all the information we'll
have about the town. We don't have any local magazines."

"Newspapers will be just fine." Nina smiled sweetly, thankful her luck was on. She had been afraid of looking too

suspicious—after all, how many tourists walked into the local library to read old newspapers—but, the librarian had given her exactly what she wanted, and Nina hadn't even asked.

The librarian nodded and led the way to a large table surrounded by shallow storage drawers. With a little more enthusiasm than she'd had when she first stepped into the library, Nina made her way to the periodical section to begin her search through back issues of the Shadow Creek *Chronicle*.

Page after page she flipped through, thinking it would be nice to have microfiche. Hours went by before she looked up at the clock in frustration. She had found nothing about an accident involving a father and daughter. Nowhere had she seen Pete Harmon's name mentioned. Nowhere had she seen her own name mentioned.

She arched backward, stretching her taut muscles. Her back popped between her shoulder blades, but it did nothing to alleviate the stress knotted there.

"Are you all right, dear? You've been sitting there an awfully long time."

Nina glanced across the room to where the librarian sat at her desk. "I'm fine," she replied politely. But she wasn't fine. Discouragement washed over her. She wasn't a detective, and her investigative ideas were limited. She'd really hoped to find some useful information in the newspaper. She hadn't thought that finding information about a car accident in such a small town was going to be difficult. Maybe she was just being naïve.

"You finding everything okay?"

"Yes—no—I mean, are there any other papers I could sift through?"

The librarian's wrinkled face cracked more as her brow furrowed. She shook her head. "Sorry, dear, the *Chronicle* is the only newspaper in Shadow Creek. Has been for years. We did get another little weekly that came out of Flagstaff, but that stopped coming . . . oh, I'd say ten or eleven years ago, maybe more. It didn't really have much about Shadow Creek, anyhow."

Nina kept her voice even. "Do you think you could tell me where to find copies of this weekly?"

"Sure, hon'. They'd be in that last drawer on the left." The librarian pointed to the drawers behind Nina. "Flagstaff *Life and Times* . . . but it doesn't have much about Shadow Creek in there."

Nina pushed the wooden chair back so fast she caught her foot on the chair leg. Stumbling backward, she caught the chair before it hit the floor.

"Oh, dear . . ." The silver-haired woman started to get up.

Nina held up a hand. "I'm all right. Really." She waited for the librarian to sit back down, and then quickly found the newspaper.

"Hitting pay dirt" wasn't exactly how Nina would have described what she found in the Flagstaff *Life and Times*. It was more like having an appetizer when you really wanted a steak. The article was small and non-descript, giving Nina only the same non-committal story she'd heard all her life. Single car accident. No witnesses. Car found by some passing tourists who stopped to look at the view. Not one mention of anyone named H. Anderson and certainly no hint of foul play.

Disappointed, Nina got out the letter and read it again. She had it almost memorized by now, but she didn't know what else to do.

Ry found Nina's convertible parked outside the library, and beads of perspiration formed on his brow. She was digging. Why else would she be at the library? Tourists didn't tend to hang out at the library. They went sightseeing, they ate expensive meals, and stayed in hotels, but they didn't go to the local library and look for a good book to curl up with.

He wiped his brow and cursed to himself. He couldn't just

walk in there and ask her what she was doing. He glanced at his watch. In a few hours, he'd have to be at work. For now, he'd have to forget about getting close to her and just keep an eye out. The mere thought of Carlucci being suspicious was frightening in itself. Ry had seen the results of crossing Carlucci, and they weren't pretty. They were headless corpses and fingerless accountants. If Carlucci thought Nina had become a threat to his operation, he wouldn't think twice about killing her.

Nina jotted down the name of the reporter who'd written the story in the *Life and Times* and decided to try to find him. Hopefully, he would be able to tell her more than what he'd written in the article. Uneasiness had already begun to envelop her. It was strange that the only paper to cover news of a motorist's death was a tiny paper fifty miles away from the scene. Especially when the local newspaper didn't think it worthy enough for a story. For that matter, the Shadow Creek *Chronicle* didn't even think it worthy of an obituary. Town reporters might well have never known the accident even happened, or so it seemed.

Going back to the Lamplighter, she called directory assistance in Flagstaff to inquire about Wilbur Chase, reporter. There was no listing. She asked for the number to the Flagstaff *Life and Times*. There was no listing.

Feeling a little dejected, Nina called the only restaurant in Shadow Creek that delivered and ordered a chef salad. Taking a deep breath, she told herself she shouldn't give up so easily. After all, it had been fifteen years. It was bound to be a little difficult to get information.

The salad arrived and while she chewed on a celery stalk, she thought about what to do next. She had one lead—an obscure article in a paper that no longer existed. Why did the Flagstaff paper run the story when the *Chronicle* didn't? How did the *Life and Times* even find out about an accident if it was so minor the local paper didn't run an article?

How could . . . It came to her, then. She dropped the half-eaten celery stalk into the clear plastic container and grabbed the local phone book. Bingo. Wilbur Chase, Sr., 101 Cherry Orchard Way.

She dialed, and a recording informed her that the number had been disconnected. She was not easily daunted. This was the first true lead she'd found. She jotted down the address and made her way to the tourists' center to pick up a map of the city.

Ry tailed Nina at a discreet distance. His Belair wasn't the most inconspicuous vehicle in the world, but it was better than a patrol car. Besides, he knew by now how to be careful.

Relieved to see her going to the tourists' center, he hoped she'd given up on Pete Harmon's death and was content to see the sights. Maybe—hopefully—he wouldn't have to worry about her at all. It was almost time to start his shift, so he turned around and went home to change. *God, don't let her mess this up.*

Chapter Five

"You're so stupid you could get run over by a bulldozer and not even know you were dead. What am I paying you for, Harper? You're supposed to know everything that goes on in that town, and you didn't even know she was there? You're useless. Do you know that? I think I'm going to make Ry the sheriff in that town. At least he knows what's going on most of the time!" Anthony Carlucci screamed into the cordless phone as he stormed through the warehouse.

He picked up a bottle of tequila out of one of the open crates and inspected it before continuing his thrashing of the Shadow Creek sheriff. "If you think I won't kill you just because you're married to my sister, you're crazy. You mess with me and you're a dead man, Harper. I told my sister not to marry trash like you."

"Tony, please. It ain't that big a deal. Now that I know she's here, I'll keep tabs on her. Settle down, will you?"

"Don't tell *me* what to do, pinhead; just do your job." Carlucci punched the OFF button and then went back to checking his latest shipment. He was so sick and tired of working with incompetents. He just might have to take out a bunch of them and get in some new and eager blood. Things just weren't the same as they used to be.

Nina rang the doorbell at 101 Cherry Orchard Way and waited for an answer. One didn't come. She rang the bell again, then beat on the door. Still no answer. She hammered the door again and a male voice bellowed, "Go away! No one's home!"

Taken aback for a moment by the unfriendly voice, Nina waited a beat before knocking again. "I'm not going away until you answer the door!" she yelled back.

"Then stay there all day for all I care!"

Nina sighed and sat on the doorstep. With her elbows on her knees, she rested her head in her hands and wondered if he'd really meant that or if he'd come to the door any minute.

Fifteen minutes later, Nina knew the answer. He was serious. She stood and rang the doorbell again. "Please open the door," she pleaded.

She peered into the window to the right of the door and met a face staring up at her. Quickly the curtain dropped, and the wrinkled face disappeared.

She knocked again and again, and still the man wouldn't answer. She had only one option—to be persistent. She knocked and knocked and continued to knock non-stop until she thought her knuckles were going to bleed.

Finally, she gave up and plopped herself back on the porch step, wondering if she would have to camp out until Wilbur Chase needed to leave the house.

Another half hour passed before the door opened. An old man in a wheelchair stared at her, his cloudy, dark eyes unyielding.

"What do you want?" he ground out. His head tremored slightly.

Nina stood up with a jolt. "Mr. Chase?" She asked.

"What do you want?"

"To talk. Can I come in?"

"Who are you, anyway?"

"Nina Thomas. I'd like to know a little bit about a story you did fifteen years ago for the Flagstaff *Life and Times*."

"What story?"

"About a man who got killed in a car accident on Shadow Creek Highway."

Chase's already pallid face paled even more. "Get away from me now!" He waved a trembling hand in her direction and then pulled back on the lever of his wheelchair and started to retreat inside.

"Please!" Nina lunged forward, slamming her hand against the door. "Yours was the only article I could find. You have to help me. Why was yours the only story?"

"I can't talk to you. I'm an old man. Go away and leave me alone. Why don't you ask the police about it? They ought to know." He slammed the door against Nina's hand and left her staring at the slab of wood.

What was she going to do now?

Ry entered the Shadow Creek sheriff's office just as Billy Ray Harper hung up the phone.

"Afternoon, Sheriff."

"How come you didn't tell me Harmon's kid's in town?" He threw Ry a black look that had absolutely no effect.

"Because this is the first time I've seen you since I found out. What's the big deal?"

"Next time you get some valuable information you'd better pick up the phone and call me, got it? I don't appreciate getting chewed up and spit out just because one of my deputies decides to go over my head."

"Yessir." He gave Harper a sarcastic salute. "Anything else wrong before I go pour myself some coffee?"

"Don't get smart with me, Andies. I got my eye on you. I don't like people who try to undermine me, so you'd better watch yourself."

"Go jump in the lake," Ry mumbled.

"What was that?"

"Yessir," Ry said aloud. He went into the back office to get a cup of coffee.

"That's what I thought you said!" Harper hollered back.

Nina left Wilbur Chase's home dejected and heartsick. Not only had she failed to uncover any information, she was even more confused than when she had started her quest. One thing that was settled in her mind was the fact that the circumstances surrounding her father's accident were a lot more complicated than she had originally anticipated. The confession from H. Anderson, the lack of news coverage about the accident, and the strange way Mr. Chase had acted when she asked about the story all added up to one big question mark. Now, all she had to do was answer the question.

Easier said than done.

Driving down the quiet residential street, Nina decided to take Mr. Chase's advice—even if he had offered it unintentionally. Maybe the police did have some files she could look at.

Ry almost dropped his coffee mug when Nina walked through the door. He couldn't have asked for an easier way to find out what she was up to. He put on his Can-I-Help-You smile. "Can I help you?" he asked her as she walked up to the counter.

He closed his mind to the sway of her hips and tried to concentrate on business. The pictures in her file really hadn't done her justice. Sure, they showed that she'd blossomed from the gangly pre-teen into a nice-looking woman, but they didn't show that, in reality, she was a true and total knockout.

She smiled at him, and he felt as if sunshine had melted all over him. *Oh, man!* He mentally shook himself. What was wrong with him? He made himself concentrate on the problem at hand—keeping them both alive and healthy.

He gave her what he hoped was a cordial smile just as she reached the counter.

"I hope so. I'm looking for some information about an accident that happened quite a few years ago. I was wondering if you would have any files I could look at."

Ry studied Nina as she read his nametag. She looked as if she might have recognized him and, for a moment, his heart stopped. Her gaze moved from his nametag to his face, and he met it straight on. Maybe she recognized him, maybe she didn't. Either way, he was going to have to play like he didn't know her from Eve.

A tentative curve formed on her lips. Then, she looked away.

Good. The wig had worked. She didn't recognize him.

He looked around to make sure Sheriff Harper was still in the bathroom. "Is it an old incident? One that would already be a matter of public record?"

"I'm pretty sure it would be." She fidgeted from one foot to the other and back again. He was glad she was nervous. It meant she was green. It meant she didn't know what she was doing. It meant she could be easily swayed. And he needed to sway her. Right out of town.

"Come this way." He ushered her down to the end of the counter and through a swinging door. "Let's go into the office, and you can give me the information."

He let her go ahead of him into the tiny room encased by walls with windows from ceiling to waist.

"Have a seat," he said, then took his place behind the scratched up wooden desk.

Nina sat in the metal chair opposite the desk. "What do I need to tell you, just the date of the accident?"

"Everything you already know, that way I can search my files more productively," Ry told her.

"Everything? Don't you have a filing system? You know, a specific subject, alphabetical by victim or accused, something simple like that?"

She was nervous, but she was also smart. Maybe he'd underestimated her. If she knew enough to hide what she knew, that didn't bode well. Ry swallowed hard. "Well, yes. We do have a system. I just thought it would be easier to know what information you needed by finding out what information you already had."

She didn't speak—just looked at him as if she were trying to figure him out, her brown eyes sparking with an apprehension that transferred to him.

Suddenly, he was as unsure as he'd been on his first assignment out of the academy. It was ridiculous, and he needed to get ahold of himself, but she made him lose all sense of logical thought. He'd known about her too long, knew her situation too well, sympathized with her too much—liked the way she looked way too much.

"Well, I don't have any information. All I know is the victim's name, the date of the accident, and where it happened."

As she relayed the information, he jotted it down as if he'd never heard of the case before. He looked up from his note pad to reassure her and noticed Harper peering in like a rabid dog through the window from across the room. Evidently, the man had finally found his way out of the john. Andies gave him a sarcastic smile and then turned his attention back to Nina.

"Why don't you give me your name, address, and phone number, and I'll call you when I've had a chance to research this. Probably won't be until tomorrow."

"I'm staying at the Lamplighter Bed & Breakfast. I don't know the number but it's on Main Street."

"I know the place." He stood. "That's all I need. I'll give you a call when I find something out."

"Thanks, Deputy," Nina replied, pushing her chair back and standing.

"Call me Ry, and don't mention it. That's what we're here for, to 'Protect and Serve,' and since this falls under the 'serve' part, it's just my job."

Deputy Andies smiled again and a sense of déjà vu flooded through Nina for a second time. She studied him with interest. She had thought he looked familiar when she'd first come in, but had dismissed the feeling. Now she wasn't so sure.

"Have we met before?" she asked.

"No. I don't think so." He met her gaze firmly and then flashed her another killer smile. "And I'm sure that I'd remember a pretty face like yours."

Nina gave him a crooked smile. Something about him made her glad she'd omitted the fact that she had a letter indicating the accident might have been deliberate. He was hiding something; she could feel it in her bones. "All right, Deputy. I'll wait to hear from you." She turned to leave and saw the sheriff staring at her. A chill coursed down her spine as their gazes met and stuck. She wanted to look away but found herself unable to break the connection. Finally, he turned, and she was released. She straightened her shoulders and tried to shrug off the unsettling feeling. "You know where to find me," she said to Andies.

"Yes, ma'am," he replied, opening the door for her.

"That was her, wasn't it?" Harper sounded like an excited toddler in a toy store, and the urge to deck him rolled over Ry in a wave.

He clenched his jaw. "Yes," he replied. *Quit drooling.*

"How'd you get her in here?"

"Why do you care? You've got what you want. Now we can keep tabs on her real easy."

"You better watch it, Andies. I'm getting sick of your high and mighty attitude. If it weren't for me, you'd have never even met Carlucci, and now he's taken a liking to you, you think you're all that. Well, let me tell you something, blood is still thicker than water. I could turn you just like that." He snapped his fingers in Andies' face.

Andies caught Harper's hand. "If you really believe that, you're an even bigger idiot than I thought. Carlucci doesn't consider you blood. He doesn't even like your blood." Ry got nose to nose with Harper. "If I were you, I'd watch my own back and stop tossing threats around like you can afford to do it."

He released Harper's hand and ran his fingers through his own hair. "I have work to do," he said then turned his back on the sheriff and left to get a sandwich. On his way out, he bumped into Jonah Martinelli, one of the other deputies. Martinelli looked at him with disgust. "Watch it, Andies."

"Aw, bite me," Andies replied, thoroughly irritated and in no mood for hassles.

If he wasn't careful, he'd end up blowing this himself. He hadn't counted on Nina showing up, on seeing her face to face. It was one thing to know *about* her and another thing entirely to *know* her. She was so innocent and hopeful. So ignorant of the trouble she was causing. He had to protect her at all costs, but it was getting difficult to keep his priorities in perspective.

He had been at this too long. He needed to get out. He needed a change of scenery—and not by way of having to fly all over the country every other day to keep tabs on everyone. He almost had Carlucci eating out of his hand, and now it looked like things were going to blow up in his face. Close to three years of work down the tubes—maybe a lifetime's, if he ended up dead.

Chapter Six

"Send Ry and Jonah down to Nogales next week," Carlucci told Harper.

"What do you mean, send Ry and Jonah? What about me?"

"I can't believe how stupid you really are. You can't go. You're the sheriff of that backward little town you live in. You can't disappear for three days. You'd be missed."

"Well everybody takes vacations, you know, Tony. I wouldn't be missed that much. Besides, I never get in on any action. I've been your brother-in-law for near twenty years. Andies hasn't even been around a dog's year, and already you treat him better'n me. How fair is that?"

"Yeah, well Ry is a lot smarter than you. He doesn't have to go around silencing witnesses. He wouldn't *have* any witnesses. It's your stupid mistakes that got us worrying about this chick roaming around town. If it weren't for you, we wouldn't even have killed her old man in the first place. But, no, you had to go and have two cops shot in broad daylight, in the middle of the road, in a town that only has—what, like three roads? You're so frigging stupid, Harper. I don't know why my sister married you."

"You don't have to get hostile, Tony. I was just askin'."

"Well, don't ask. From now on just do what you're told without asking, got it?"

"Got it, Tony. I'll tell Andies and Martinelli to go down to Nogales next week, right?"

"Right. Tell them it's the last house before the Mexican border. It'll be a good raid for them."

"How're we gonna justify our bust to the Nogales police?" Harper asked.

"Do I have to come up with every little detail for you? Arizona's open jurisdiction. Just tell them some bogus story about being there on vacation or something. I don't care; just get my shipment back fast so I can sell it again."

"Okay, Tony. Don't worry. We'll take care of it," Harper assured him.

Ry parked his patrol car outside Ma & Pa's diner. Ma was the only one running the place since Pa had died a few years back, and she greeted Andies with a bear hug and a smile.

"Hiya, Ry. You've been away a while. What's the matter? Don't you like my cooking anymore?"

He held the hefty woman at arm's length and filled his lungs. That was one thing about Ma Spooner, her bear hugs could squeeze the life out of anyone.

"Of course I still like your cooking, Ma. I was just away on business for a few days. Think you could fix me some of your famous biscuits and gravy?"

"For you, darlin', anything." She pinched his cheek. "Even if it ain't time for breakfast." She turned and eased her overweight body behind the counter, yelling back, "Take your usual place, sweetie, and I'll have your lunch in a jiffy."

Ry sat at a booth midway down the wall and peered out

onto Main Street. The road was almost empty, and he wondered, not for the first time, how the town stayed alive.

"Madge is back from Phoenix." Ma continued to talk from across the room.

Ry turned his head and gave the older woman a crooked smile. Ma Spooner had been trying to get him to marry her daughter ever since he'd "strode into town," as she liked to phrase it. In Ry's mind, Madge was too young—only nineteen—and unlike her mother, too skinny. Her stomach was a cavity between two protruding hipbones, and her throat looked almost skeletal. In addition to her anorexic appearance, she was a neverending flirt, throwing herself at every man that came through the door of the diner. Even if he hadn't been undercover, there was nothing really appealing about Madge.

Nina, on the other hand. Nina was already under his skin. He hadn't realized how much until she'd come flesh-and-blood into his life. He'd always been close to her in his mind. He really had no choice. They were connected in ways that most people never were. He knew her life as he knew his own. And it had been fine as long as all he knew was in his head and in a file.

Now it was different. Now, he'd looked into her eyes. Beautiful eyes. Innocent eyes. Eyes that needed his help. He mentally shook himself. *Forget about her eyes, Ry.*

Ma brought over a pot of coffee and turned over the mug already on the table. "Biscuits be ready in a minute," she said.

"Thanks, Ma."

Ry took a sip of his coffee just as the door chimes sounded. He looked up to see Nina coming through the door. He smiled and waved her over.

Ma, who had been scurrying over to greet the pretty stranger, stopped dead in her tracks. *Now the whole town's going to think I'm dating her,* Ry thought.

"Hello, Deputy," Nina said.

"It's Ry, remember. Please, sit down."

"Thanks." She sat in the booth opposite him and smiled. "Don't suppose you've had time to find anything out?"

"No," he confessed. "But I will."

"It's been such a long time, I know it's going to be difficult," she told him.

Ma came over and offered Nina a menu and a cup of coffee. Nina accepted both with a smile, but Ma didn't return the gesture. She just sized Nina up and down, gave Ry a disapproving look, and then waddled down the aisle and across to the counter.

Nina's brow furrowed. "What did I do?"

Ry chuckled. "Nothing. She just thinks your ruining her daughter's chances of becoming my wife. Don't worry about it. Her chances were slim to none before you sat down." He took a sip of his coffee.

He shook his head. "So have you found anything out yet, yourself?"

"I told you, officer, I'd already given you all the information I have. Don't you believe me?"

"Of course I believe you, and call me Ry. It's just that it seems a little strange to me that you would come in search of answers so long after the accident. Something must have prompted you."

"No. Not really." She shrugged. "When I was a kid, a friend of mine told me about this accident. She'd lived in Shadow Creek for a while and told me about some crazy Vietnam vet who went nuts and killed himself and his little girl. I was fascinated and wanted to know more."

Boy, that tale would have made the Brothers Grimm proud. "But what took you so long?" Ry played along with her story. She could tell a good one. She'd have been pretty convincing if he hadn't already known who she really was.

She sipped on her water, staring into the glass. When she put the glass back on the table, she looked him dead in the eye. "Just life, really. I've been trying to find time away from school and work to take the opportunity. And I finally did."

"What are you studying?" Ry asked, as if he didn't already know everything there was to know about her.

"Law," Nina said, taking him by surprise.

"Law?" That's not what he'd been told.

She nodded.

"You don't seem like the lawyer type to me. Seems like you ought to be a teacher, or something like that." *That's* what he'd been told. When had she quit studying education, and why was his intel messed up? What else could be wrong?

He couldn't think about that.

"Well, I was studying special education, but recently I decided to change my major. It's a little bit of a setback as far as getting my degree goes, but I don't mind."

"What made you change your mind?" He sipped his coffee, but his gaze never left her.

Nina studied Ry's face. It was an honest face, she decided, and it wasn't just because a cop's uniform came with it that she thought so. Sure, at first she'd thought he was hiding something, but now there was something honest and caring in his eyes. It made her want to tell him about the letter. She opened her mouth then closed it again.

What if her first instinct had been right?

She thought for a moment and then decided to test him. If he passed, she would trust him. If he didn't . . . well, she wasn't sure what she'd do, but she wouldn't tell him about the letter. That was for sure.

She inhaled a deep breath and lifted a nonchalant shoulder, trying to look relaxed. "I don't know. I think because I've heard so much stuff about dirty cops. They're just as bad as criminals, if not worse. Don't you agree? I'd like to see some of them get their just desserts."

Nina studied his reaction carefully. She wasn't a professional detective, but she figured if he protested her insult too much, she could take it as a sign to at least be cautious. She really needed an ally, and the deputy seemed like a good one, but not if he really had something to hide.

But, he didn't even flinch at her insinuation, so he either was honest or was a consummate liar. And she was right back where she was before her little ruse—with no way to know if he could be trusted.

"I'm sure there aren't as many dirty cops as the media portrays. Take me, for example." He smiled again.

"Are you sure we've never met?" Nina asked. She squinted in order to get a better look.

His smile faded. "No. We've never met." He started to slide over in the booth. "Well, I really have to be getting back to work now. It's been nice talking to you, and I'll call you when I have some information."

He reached across the table and shook her hand and then left the restaurant just as Ma Spooner brought his biscuits and gravy to the table. She looked at the closing door in confusion. "What happened? He get a call or something?" she asked Nina.

"I don't know," Nina replied, peering out the window, to watch Ry drive away.

"You want to order?"

"No thank you." Nina started to leave, but Ma detained her.

"You want to eat his biscuits and gravy?"

"No. No, thank you. I must be going. How much do I owe you for the coffee?"

Ma looked at Nina's untouched cup. "Nothing."

"Oh. What about the deputy's, then?"

"He don't have to buy his coffee in here. We all like the deputy mighty fine."

"Well, then, thank you again." Nina tried to get up, but Ma was still standing in the way. "I really must be going now."

Evidently, Ma didn't take the hint.

"You be careful about Ry. He's dear to us all, and we don't want no strangers runnin' through town hurtin' his feelin's. Understand?"

"Oh, indubitably," Nina replied.

"Huh?"

"Yes, yes. I understand completely. Now, can I go please?"

Ma Spooner moved aside, and Nina scurried out the door as fast as she could, convinced people in this town were insane. Deputies ran like scared rabbits for no apparent reason, restaurant owners did all but threaten your life, and wheelchair-bound old men locked their doors when you mentioned an accident that happened more than a decade ago.

She'd be glad to get home.

"You and Martinelli have to go to Nogales next week," Harper relayed to Ry.

"Who are we busting?"

"Don't know. Tony just said to be at the—what was it again?" He shuffled through a clutter of papers and pulled one out from the middle. "Last house before the Mexican border."

"Yeah, but who lives there." Ry snatched the paper from Harper. The sheriff's ignorance was starting to grate on his nerves. Little by little, every day, his patience was wearing thin.

And that was not a healthy sign.

"I don't know, I told you. Why'd you ask me all these stupid questions? Who cares, anyway? Just get down there and pick up the shipment."

Andies stuck the note in his pants pocket. "You're a real pain in the—"

"Yeah, I know it. It's my specialty." Harper walked away, then disappeared into his private office—the john.

Andies followed him to the door and knocked. "I'm going home for a minute. I'll be right back."

"Hey, you keeping tabs on that Thomas chick?" Harper yelled back.

"Yeah. I know her every move. Don't worry."

Chapter Seven

Smoke filled the sky in angry black billows. The road stretched out silently, except for the wailing of children and the crying of men and women. Even with her car windows rolled up, Nina could hear the firemen yelling to one another. A baby screamed wildly; it sounded as if someone were bludgeoning it. Nina tried to seek out the child. A woman, her face streaked with soot, stood in sullied clothing clutching the whimpering infant to her bosom. Violently she rocked the child, moving faster with each screaming crescendo.

"Get another hose, quick!" somebody yelled. Nina searched and finally focused on where the fire was coming from.

The Lamplighter Bed & Breakfast was a blaze of towering flames, the guest rooms reduced to smoldering timber.

Horrified, Nina got out of her car and started walking toward the blaze.

"Nina, don't go any closer."

She looked down at the arm barred gently across her chest, then followed the arm up to its shoulder to see Ry standing in front of her.

"What happened?" she asked.

"We don't know yet. I was just on my way home and I heard the call come in. I guess it's a good thing you weren't here."

"Is anyone hurt? Are Mags and Harvey okay?"

"They're fine. The main building hasn't been touched. We've got a couple of casualties—smoke inhalation, cuts and bruises, that sort of thing. Luckily, nobody was killed."

"Thank God. What happened? How did it start?"

"We don't know yet."

"Oh, I already asked you that, didn't I? I'm sorry."

"Don't worry about it." Ry took her arm and led her to his patrol car. "Sit here, and I'll be back in a minute." She sank onto the gray velour seat. Red and blue reflected intermittently on the passenger window of the squad car. She focused on the reflection for a moment, then turned back to Officer Andies—Ry.

"What about my things? Are they . . . are they . . . are they all gone?"

"I don't know for sure, Nina, but I wouldn't get my hopes up," he said softly. He glanced toward the fire and then back at her before turning his gaze back to the fire. She sensed he was torn between leaving her alone and going to help. Odd that he would be torn, but she somehow took comfort in that.

"I'll be right back." he finally said and then moved toward the blaze.

Only a few moments later, he returned to check on her. "You okay?"

She nodded slowly, her gaze never leaving the throng of victims and concerned citizens that milled about. She felt robotic, her joints stiff, her muscles tight, but her mind was a whir with all the activity. What if she'd been in her room? The thought electrified her every nerve, and she suddenly felt completely spent. What if she'd been in her room? *What if I was* meant *to be in my room?*

"Here, drink some of this. It will make you feel better." Ry handed her a paper cup of water, and she sipped on it obediently before giving back an empty cup.

"Try to rest a bit, and I'll be back in a little while. Okay?"

She nodded.

In the growing dusk, the firemen looked like frenzied silhouettes as Nina sat in the patrol car, peering at them through the open door. She still couldn't believe that all her belongings were now just flakes of ash. Nausea rolled her stomach as the realization hit her. What was she going to do now? Go home to an empty house with questions still unanswered? What choice did she have? Buy new clothes? She didn't think her meager salary could handle that added expense, and it had taken her entire savings to make the trip in the first place. If only her parents hadn't been away on vacation. They could have Fed-Exed more clothes. Now she had no choice but to just go home herself.

She rested her head on the back of the seat as the tears begin to trickle down her cheeks. She swiped them away and then wrapped her arms around her body as far as they would reach. It wasn't cold outside, but somehow, she was starting to chill. The finality of her unfinished journey seemed imminent, and the despair drained her. She closed her eyes to avoid looking at the people, the flashing lights, the stretchers. She closed her ears to the shouts and cries and tried to forget about the terrible aftermath she would have to face tomorrow. Pulling her knees to her chest, she maneuvered her body to a comfortable position.

She just needed to rest.

Ry drove Nina to his house. The fire chief had already determined the blaze was arson. Traces of benzol had been found all over one of the rooms—Nina's room—and Ry found himself feeling a little more protective than he should. His main concern had always been keeping her safe, but now he needed to keep her oblivious to the fact that she'd been the target of the Lamplighter fire. Things were going from bad to worse, and he knew if he couldn't resolve this whole thing in a hurry, corpses were going to start popping up like daffodils in spring.

He glanced over at her, asleep in the passenger seat. She looked so innocent. He didn't know what her reaction would be when she realized he'd taken her home. She wasn't going to approve, he was sure of it, but he really didn't feel like there was any other choice. He couldn't let her out of his sight. Not now. Not after tonight.

Lancelot was going to have a field day when he found out about this. Ry wasn't looking forward to telling him.

And Rich. Rich was going to go ballistic.

Ry sighed and pulled the car into the driveway. He kept his eye on Nina through the windshield as he rounded the front of the vehicle and moved to the passenger door. Sleeping, she looked as if she didn't have a care in the world. He wished she didn't.

He really hated his job. He couldn't even remember why he'd chosen it in the first place. Well, that wasn't exactly true. He could remember. It was because of his dad. It was because he wanted to protect the innocent, fight for justice, rid the world of evil. But all those reasons seemed trite and irrelevant now. His dad was gone, and Ry had had to align himself with evil so many times over the years that he wasn't even sure anymore if he was a good guy or a bad one.

Looking at Nina reminded him of that. Under different circumstances, he could've started something good with her. At least, he thought he could. She was decent. Caring. Trusting. What would she do when she found out he'd been lying to her all along? What would she say if she ever found out about his connection to her father's murder? He was definitely a bad guy—even if he were playing on the good guy team.

He released the latch on the car door and gently swept her into his arms. She focused on his face for a moment and then closed her eyes. He could tell she didn't comprehend who he was or where he was taking her.

He fumbled with his keys, trying not to wake her as he opened the door. She stirred slightly and nuzzled against his shoulder. He put his face to her hair. She smelled like fresh flowers. "Please trust me," he whispered.

He nudged open the front door with his knee. The hallway was dimly aglow from the streetlight as Ry made his way to the bedroom. Limply, Nina lay cradled in his arms as he crossed the room and laid her on one side of the bed.

He was turning down the covers when she peeked at him through half-open lids. "Officer . . . Ry?" she mumbled.

"Shh. Go back to sleep. You've had a rough night. We'll talk in the morning," he whispered.

"Mmm." Nina slept.

Ry took off her shoes and moved her under the covers. He grabbed yesterday's shirt and pants off the chair and stuffed them into the laundry hamper by the door, then grabbed some pajamas and went into the living room.

Emptying his pockets onto the table, he found the paper he'd taken from Harper about the trip to Nogales. *Next week,* he thought. *Next week this will all be over.* He read the sheriff's scribblings—*Wed Tony Nogales 2nd house 500 key deposit.*— then put the note on the bookshelf inside a volume of *War and Peace.*

When Nina awoke, the trees outside were shadow dancing on the striped wallpaper. Confused, she studied her surroundings, trying to place herself. This room was in no way familiar. It was a masculine room. Thick-striped wallpaper in heavy blue. An old dark wood dresser with no sort of decoration whatsoever. A bare chair. Where was she?

A knock on the door startled her and, clutching the covers to her chin, she let out a meek, "Come in."

Ry strode through the door clad in jeans and a polo shirt, and Nina's stomach gave her a one-two punch. The memory of the fire spilled over her, and the blood rushed from her face. She had lost everything. She smiled tentatively and tried to meet Ry's eyes.

"Good morning," he said, placing the tray on the bedside table. "Are you ready for some nice, hot breakfast and a steaming cup of coffee?"

The aroma immediately made Nina hungry, and she scooted to a sitting position, still clutching the sheets to her chin.

Ry looked at her and smiled. "You're fully clothed under there, you know? Unless, of course, you undressed yourself in the middle of the night."

Nina lifted the covers and peeked underneath. Her face warmed, and she looked at Ry. "I knew that." She smiled and arranged the covers around her lap. "The breakfast smells delicious, and I really appreciate it, but why am I here? I assume this is your house?"

"Yes, it's mine. You're here because you were asleep when I got back to the car last night, and I didn't know what else to do with you."

"Oh . . . well . . ." Awkwardness draped the room in silence. She didn't know what to say, so she blurted out the first thing that came to mind, "Well, things could be worse. I could've been in the room, I suppose."

"I know you're being sarcastic, but it's true, Nina. You could've been there. Having your life spared is nothing to sneeze at."

"I know. I know." She gave him a slight nod. "It's just that I had really wanted to find something out about that accident, and now I don't know if I'll be able to stay. I can't afford to buy new clothes, my parents are—oh, everything I needed was in that . . ." She stopped short. Ry was a complete stranger; what was she doing telling him?

A crushing realization shattered Ry inside as he listened to Nina explain her dilemma. What if the arsonist hadn't gotten what he was after? Ry couldn't decide if her being forced to leave town made him happy or sad. He wanted her out of the way. With her snooping around, his job became a hundred times more lethal. It was better if she went home with her tail between her legs. But what if it didn't end there? What if they'd actually been trying to kill her? He wouldn't put it past Carlucci, even for a second, and if that were the case, they would come after her again as soon as they found out she was still alive. No. He couldn't let her leave. He had to keep her with him until this whole thing was over. It was the only way he'd know for sure she was safe.

"Don't you have any family who can lend you some money?" he asked.

"No. My parents don't even know—I mean, they're away on vacation."

"You can't call them?" He didn't want to put the idea in her head—all he needed was more people showing up—but he did need to sound as if he were truly trying help.

Nina shrugged. "I didn't bring their travel schedule with me." She looked down. "I guess I'm going home."

The thought came to his mind again that home might be the best place for her, but Ry dismissed it immediately. Problem was, he wasn't sure if he dismissed it because she really was in danger, or because he just wanted her close to him.

"Look," he said, "I'll loan you some money so you can go and buy a few things, and you can stay here as long as you like."

For several moments, Nina just stared at him. Then she blinked. Slowly, she shook her head. "I'm sorry, but I could never take money from you—or stay in your house. I don't even know you."

"Sure you do," he said easily. "I'm your knight in shining armor." He laughed, but Nina didn't. "Okay," he said. "You know I'm a cop in this town. Trustworthy." He took a step toward her. "Right?"

Her expression softened, and she looked him directly in the eyes. It did strange things to his gut that he chose to ignore.

"Why do you want to help me? Isn't it a little above and beyond the call?"

He didn't answer straight away. He was afraid the truth might flow out of his mouth. Never in a million years would he have believed he'd have Pete Harmon's daughter in his home, let alone be trying to convince her to stay there. Lancelot was going to pop his cork when he found out. Ry could already hear the "against procedure" speech. But what else was he supposed to do? Carlucci didn't seem quite as amiable about her as he had before she'd shown up in Shadow Creek. He wanted to kill her and get on with it—*would* kill her, if she seemed the least bit suspicious.

Ry had only one viable choice: keep her right underfoot where he could protect her before she got caught in another deliberate accidental fire.

"Look, I'm not sure why you decided to come to this rat hole of a town, but I'm willing to guess you haven't gotten what you came for. If your family's out of town and you've lost all your money and belongings, you've got two choices. Take money from me and leave town, without whatever it is you wanted, or take money from me and stay. What's it going to be?"

Nina chewed on her bottom lip. She didn't want to take money from a stranger, and she wanted to stay in his house even less. But she really didn't have much of a choice, not with her mother and stepfather on vacation and out of touch. She'd cleared out her savings to make this trip and most of that money had been hidden in the hotel room. What was she supposed to do? She studied Ry's face. That face she'd deemed honest just yesterday. She didn't think he'd try to harm her in any way; he didn't look like the sort. And she didn't really want to go home. Not with all the questions surrounding her father's death still unanswered.

Things were just starting to look good. She'd found that reporter—and he'd acted awfully strange, as if he had something to hide. There were definitely things to be discovered in Shadow Creek. And she wanted to know what those things were.

"All right," she finally said. "But it's only for a few days. I'll think of something by then."

He pulled his wallet out of his back pocket and handed her two hundred dollars. "This ought to be enough to get you some new clothes."

Nina reluctantly took the money, still not comfortable with the arrangement even though she thought it her best option. "Thank you," she said quietly. "I don't know how I can ever repay you."

"With cash," Ry smiled.

Nina laughed. "Touché. Now hand over that food. I'm starved."

Chapter Eight

"She's at the house? *Your* house? Are you insane?"

"Calm down, Lance. I figured it's the best place for her. Especially since someone—and we know who that someone is—just tried to make toast out of her."

"I just can't condone it. It's too dangerous—for everybody. If Carlucci *is* trying to kill her, then you don't want her around. It might blow your cover. And if he was just trying to scare her, he might get the impression that you're protecting her, and *that* might blow your cover. No, Anderson, no. It's against procedure. Get her out of there, and go about your business. You're no good to us dead."

"C'mon, Lancelot . . ."

"Don't call me that when you're trying to butter me up. It won't work. I'm Special Agent Lance E. Lottawalski right now, and your boss, so get her out. Got it?"

"Yes, boss. I've got it, but it's not going to be easy. She doesn't have anywhere else to go."

"Give me a break. There's more than one hotel in that stupid little town."

"Yeah, but everyone else at the Lamplighter had to find another place too. It isn't like any of them are real big places. She'll be lucky to find a room in the basement."

"Blast it, Anderson! How could you be so stupid? As you're so fond of reminding me, you're not a rookie. Don't you have common sense enough not to house someone we're tailing at your own place?"

"It's not that bad."

"What is it? You got the hots for her or something? . . ."

"Give me more credit than that," Ry said, but he knew he was lying. He only hoped Lance didn't know.

"Yeah, well you'd better watch yourself. You lay one hand on her and Rich'll cut it off. He wants Carlucci bad, and if you screw it up, he'll come after you with a hatchet."

"I got to go. She's just coming in the door. I don't want her to hear us talking."

"Okay, but listen here—"

Ry hung up before Lottawalski could finish his sentence. Man, he'd be glad when this was all over.

The phone rang almost immediately. He checked the caller I.D. and grabbed the receiver. "Speak."

" 'Bout time you got off the phone. What have you been doing?"

"What do you want?" Harper's whiny voice always set Ry on edge, and after getting chewed out by Lance, he really wasn't in the mood.

"Carlucci's ticked. He thought that wench'd leave town after last night's mishap, but she's still here—on a shopping spree, no less."

Ry knew exactly where Nina was. She'd left the house two hours ago, and had walked back in thirty minutes ago. She'd spent most of the time at the grocery store. She'd had lunch at the Lamplighter. No library. No snooping. Just shopping.

"Yeah. So what does he want *me* to do about it?" he said to Harper.

"He didn't get specific. He just wants you to take care of it."

"I wonder sometimes how you guys made it without me. He expects me to do everything. Next he'll want me to . . . never mind." He looked around to make sure Nina wasn't coming down the hall. "She's not hurting anything. I don't know why he's so worried about her."

"I don't know either, Ry, but I wouldn't talk like that about Tony if I were you." Harper's feigned concern didn't fool Ry. He knew Harper would just as soon see him dead as give him the time of day.

"Tell him that I have everything under control, and he doesn't have to worry about her, okay?"

"Whatever you say, Ry. Just make sure you're sure of whatever it is you're doing, 'cause if you ain't, and Tony gets screwed, I'll be leading your funeral procession." Harper laughed and began to hum the "Death March."

Andies slammed down the receiver. The sooner he got this assignment over with, the better.

He went in search of Nina and found her in the kitchen. "You didn't have to buy food, you know. I lent you that money for clothes and stuff." He leaned on the doorjamb.

Nina peeped over the top of the open refrigerator door and set her thick-fringed gaze on him. Her eyes never failed to captivate him. "I know," she said, "but it's not as if I didn't have *any* money of my own—just not enough to buy a new wardrobe—and since you're being so generous with your home, the least I could do was furnish some food and cooking. Although I have to warn you, I'm not a very good cook."

She stuck her hand into the plastic sack on the counter and pulled out a bag of apples, then turned and dropped the fruit into the crisper drawer. She moved gracefully, fluidly, as if she belonged in his kitchen, and he found himself thinking how nice it would be if—

"Is work a pain?"

"Huh?"

"Work. Is it irritating? You didn't sound very happy on the phone."

"You heard that?" It was the douse of cold reality he needed to put himself in check. He had a job to do here. He needed to stay focused.

Focus. He turned. Blinked. Forced an answer. "Just a rough couple of days."

"I wasn't prying, I—"

"I didn't say you were."

"I mean I didn't hear your conversation. I just heard your tone of voice. Understand?" She sounded guilty, and that worried him.

He reran the conversations in his head. Had he said anything incriminating? He didn't think so. He told himself to relax. "I understand. Don't worry about it." He forced a smile.

Nina spun back to the refrigerator. The groceries were already put away, but she had to separate herself from Ry, even if it was just by turning her back on him. It disturbed her that she found him appealing. Just one smile from him, and she wanted to tell him everything, the entire story. All about her dreams as a kid. All about the letter from H. Anderson. All about the weird way Wilbur Chase had acted when she'd asked about his article.

It was crazy. She wasn't even a trusting person. She'd always been wary of others. She supposed it was because of her childhood dreams. They had always confused her. Made her feel as if she were insane, so she had always been reserved around others, worrying that they would discover the insanity she was trying to hide and then reject her.

She shook the notion of confiding in him from her mind. Sure, he seemed honest, had taken her in, helped her in a time of need, had a killer smile that turned her legs to jelly, but she didn't really know him, and she had to be careful. If her father really had been murdered, she needed not to trust anyone. She glanced over her shoulder and found Ry looking at her. He didn't seem old enough to have known her father, but he had gotten awfully defensive when he thought she'd overheard his conversation. What did he have to hide?

She closed her eyes, suddenly afraid, suddenly helpless.

"You okay? You look like someone died or something."

"I'm fine." She hustled across the room and shouldered past him and into the hall.

He reached out and put a hand on her arm. "You sure?"

"Yes. Quite sure." She made her way down the corridor to the bedroom. She was numb. Thoughts swirled. Her father's face swam before her mind. The faceless image of the unknown H. Anderson joined her father's. Both lay lifeless in a black abyss. The image of the Lamplighter Bed & Breakfast hot and ablaze burned into her mind. What if the fire hadn't been an accident? Were they coming for her now?

Her blood ran cold. She needed answers. She needed help, but who could she trust?

Ry knocked on the door. "Nina," he said, through the closed door, "if you need to talk, I'm all ears. I might not be able to help much, but I'm a top-rate listener." He knocked again. "Nina?"

"Really. It's nothing. I just . . . I mean . . . Things are not going well." Tears stung the backs of her eyes, and she trapped the drops behind squeezed lids. She sank onto the bed. She needed guidance. She needed hope. Neither seemed within reach.

"Let me in, Nina. It might help to talk."

She didn't answer. She couldn't let him in.

The stricken look on Nina's face as she had hurried past him and down the hall worried Ry. He gave the door a perfunctory knock then turned the knob. She hadn't locked the door. That was a plus. He gave it a tiny shove and took a step across the threshold. She was sitting on the bed with her arms wrapped around herself so tightly her fingertips were outlined in white. He didn't know what had upset her, but he knew he wanted to fix it.

He was treading on shaky ground here. He knew it, but he couldn't turn back now. Nor did he want to. She wasn't just a name and a statistic from some long ago case. She was real. As real as the danger she was in. As real as the danger he was in because of her.

He had to get her out of this.

He had to get himself out of it.

He hoped he could.

"Nina?" His voice sounded funny to his ears, so quiet, so hollow. He wondered if she'd heard him. She didn't move, just continued to stare at some spot on the carpet.

He eased his way across the room and sat down next to her. The bed sank under his weight and shifted Nina a little. Still she didn't look at him.

"I didn't expect it to be this difficult."

He wanted to take her in his arms, reassure her that he had everything under control, but he knew he couldn't do that. Instead, he laced his fingers together and rested his hands on his lap. "Whatever it is, I'm sure it will all work out in the end." It was a lame thing to say, he knew, but something better escaped him.

Turning to him slightly, she looked directly into his eyes. "I don't know anymore. I just don't know. Investigating this accident has turned out to be a nightmare that I can't seem to wake up from."

He didn't know what to say. It was so difficult, knowing more about her than he should, but also not knowing enough to keep her out of harm's way. He wished she'd confide in him, tell him exactly what she knew. Then maybe he'd be able to do something useful.

He looked into her lonely, sad eyes. She was fighting off tears. Her eyes glistened like reflections bouncing off puddles in the street. She pulled at his heart, and he didn't like it—or maybe he liked it too much.

He showed her a smile. "You want to tell me about it?"

He watched her throat move as she swallowed, and then the tears welled in her eyes once more. "Everything's going wrong."

The anguish in her tone made his want to hold her return. He pushed it away and forced himself to sound nonchalant. "What do you mean?"

She handed him her cell phone. "My phone is dead."

That was the last thing he expected her to say, and he wasn't sure how to respond.

She looked at him with a rheumy gaze. She blinked, and a single tear dripped out and hung on her bottom lash. "My charger was in the hotel room."

She slapped away the tear and shook her head as if to clear it. She gave him a slight smile. "You must think I'm a real fool. It's just been a rough couple of weeks. I'm sorry. I'm not usually a blubbering fool."

Strong. Beautiful. Gutsy. That's what he thought of her, but he couldn't tell her that. "If you need to make a call, you can use my phone, you know. We might be able to find you a replacement charger, but looking at this thing, I don't think so. Smart phones haven't quite made their way to Shadow Creek yet. You'll have to head into Flag for that. I'm on duty here for the next few days, but I can take you in then if you want."

She shrugged. "I don't think so. I've got two more at home. I'm being silly, I know. I guess the fire at the Lamplighter just shook me up a little more than I thought."

He wasn't surprised. It had done the same thing to him, and he wasn't even the target. If she had even the slightest hint of what was going on, he could only imagine the things that had gone through her mind.

Ry was being so understanding, but he was still a stranger and didn't know how important this trip was to her. He didn't know it was her father who had died. He didn't know that it wasn't an accident. He didn't know that she had been there, and that she felt horribly guilty for not being able to remember one fraction of what had happened—and she should remember. It was her responsibility to remember. Especially if someone had murdered her father.

She had failed him fifteen years ago, and she was failing him now. Every avenue was a dead end—every pool full of quicksand. She could feel her will being suffocated in the murky swirl of unanswered questions. It was obvious to her now that something sinister had happened, and somebody knew about it. However, finding *that* somebody and getting them to tell *that* something was proving to be insurmountable.

Wilbur Chase knew something; that truth ached in her bones and wouldn't go away. He could help her but refused.

A wave of nausea suddenly gripped her. She swayed, started to tip over. Then Ry grabbed her.

"Are you all right?"

Nina tried to focus on his face. Such a nice face. Her head throbbed. She forced herself to focus. "I'm fine. I think I'm just worn out from everything that's happened."

"You sure you don't want to talk about what's got you so shook up?"

She shook her head.

"Okay, lie down for a little while. Your body could probably use the rest."

"Maybe you're right."

Ry scooted her to the head of the bed and gently urged her to lie down.

"You rest," he told her. He covered her with the patchwork quilt from the bottom of the bed, and then left her alone.

Slumber came quickly to Nina's weary body.

"Lance, we've got a little problem."

"What else could possibly be wrong?"

"Nina had contact with Dad."

"What do you mean *contact*?"

"She was pretty shook up this afternoon. I'm not sure why, but after she fell asleep, I found a letter from Dad. That's why she's here. He must've mailed it before he died. I didn't get to read it because I didn't want to chance waking her, but I recognized his handwriting."

Lottawalski let out a curse that traveled through the phone lines.

"And it was postmarked from Virginia."

"Was he trying to get her killed? I don't know what happened to that man."

"He was a good man, once, Lance."

"I'm sorry, Ry. I didn't mean anything by that. He was one of my best friends once."

Ry let out a sigh. "I know it."

"How much does she know?" He cursed again. "You'd better take things real slow, Ry, or you're going to mess up this whole thing."

"I know. Well, I better go. I don't want her to catch me on the phone."

"Keep in contact, Rylan. Close contact, got it?"

"Yes, Lance. Don't worry about me. I'm a big boy, and I can take care of myself."

"Well, it's not you I'm worried about; it's her. Lay low. Hopefully we'll be out of this in a week."

Ry made it home after his shift to find Nina on her way out the door.

"Going somewhere?"

"Back to this old man's house that I met to find out if he'll tell me anything." She backed up to let him in.

So, she'd found out about Wilbur. That wasn't good. "About what?" he asked her.

"About the accident. What else?"

"Oh. But I thought I was investigating that for you."

"Well, you were, or you are, but so far you haven't given me any information."

"I have been rather busy, what with recent events and all." He touched her arm and tried to guide her to the sofa. He didn't need her poking around.

She didn't budge. "I know. I wasn't complaining. It's just that I have to get some answers soon."

"It's an old case. What's so urgent about it?"

She seemed to hesitate for a moment, and then she walked over to the sofa and sat down. She stared at the floor. "I lied," she said softly.

He didn't speak, just waited for her to elaborate. At last he was getting somewhere with her. He only hoped it meant she trusted him.

She looked him straight in the eye. "I'm sorry. The accident. I wasn't told about it by a friend. It was my mother who told me. Told me over and over.

"The man who died in that accident was my father. My parents were divorced when I was very young. I lived with my father. The day he died, I was on my way to go live with my mother."

"Why?" A stab of guilt pricked Ry's conscience at having to pretend he didn't already know.

She glanced down for a moment, and when she looked on him again, the twisted grief on her face reached down his throat and ripped out his heart. He burned to tell her everything he knew. To comfort her somehow. But he couldn't.

It was against procedure.

"I don't know." Her voice broke along with his heart. "I don't remember."

He couldn't stand it anymore. Forget procedure! He closed the distance between them and wrapped her in his arms. He didn't know what to expect, but he was surprised—relieved—when she collapsed against him, allowing him to carry all her weight. Gladly he took it—her physical weight and her emotional weight. He caressed her hair. "Stay here," he said softly.

He closed his eyes and inhaled the lingering flowery scent of her shampoo. The desire to hold her forever washed over him, and he closed his eyes, willing it away. He needed to keep his wits about him. He couldn't care for her. It would make him careless, and he couldn't afford to be careless.

She shifted in his arms, just slightly, and he pulled her just a little tighter. She needed this—the reassurance of safety, he told himself. But he wasn't really buying it. *He* needed this. He needed her. He wasn't even sure why. He just knew he did.

Man, he was in trouble.

Nina could feel his breath on her hair, feel the soft caress of his hands on each strand, and for the first time since the Lamplighter had burned, she felt safe. Felt hope. There was something about him that made her want to trust him, even though she knew she shouldn't. And as she rested in the safety of his arms, she felt strangely at peace. It was a feeling she had searched for her entire life, and one she never thought to own. Peace. Security. Rightness.

It was both welcome and frightening, all at the same time. Logic told her to be cautious. She didn't even know this man, but her heart refused to listen. It ached to reach out to him, to yield everything into his guardianship.

"Stay here," he said again, "and I'll investigate everything and tell you what I can. You won't have to lift a finger. Don't worry. I'll take care of it for you. I'll do it. I'll do it all."

"But . . ."

"Shh," he said gently then slowly shifted her to face him. "You've had a rough couple of days, what with losing most of your things in the fire and not even having your family around to help you deal with it. Just rest up, take it easy, and I'll pool what information I can for you."

She studied his face and saw only sincerity. "Why are you doing this? Helping me?"

He smiled down at her. "Because you asked me to."

That was true, Nina thought. She had walked into the sheriff's office and asked for help. Maybe she should let him do it. Maybe he could easily get her the answers she needed. She thought about the letter in her purse. She trusted Ry. Trusted him maybe more than she should, but she couldn't help herself.

It just felt right.

Nina sighed. "All right."

He smiled. "Okay."

Her gaze locked with his, and time stood still in the silence. For a moment, she thought she saw uncertainty flicker across his face, but it dissolved into something else. Slowly, he lowered his head, until his face was only a fraction of an inch from hers. Her pulse quickened as the desire for his kiss met her every cell.

"Nina?" His voice was almost a whisper, the timbre resonating through her like ripples of warm water.

"Ry."

"You trust me, don't you?"

"Yes," she murmured.

Ry ignored the sliver of guilt that gnawed at his conscience and lost himself in Nina. He touched his lips to hers and watched her eyes flutter closed as she sank against him. She felt like heaven in his arms. He deepened the kiss, felt her sway, but then she pulled back a little. Their lips separated, and he felt as if he'd just had the wind knocked out of him.

He studied her, silently asked why. Time stretched, and then she spoke. "I need to tell you something."

He didn't want to release her, but he knew he had to. He nodded his approval, knowing that if he tried to speak, he'd betray everything he felt for her. She gently pulled herself away from his embrace, but he stayed her, not wanting to let her go just yet. He found his voice. "Wait one minute." She waited, met his gaze, as his blood raced through his veins. He didn't really have anything to say, he just hadn't wanted to let her go.

"What is it?" Suddenly there was worry behind her eyes. That wasn't what he'd intended. He swallowed hard.

"Nothing," he said softly. He leaned forward and pressed his lips to her forehead. "Nothing," he said again. He cradled her face in his hands and tasted her lips one more brief time. "Just trust me, okay? Don't worry." He released her, but she didn't move.

"I trust you, Ry. Really, I do. You'll see."

And she told him everything. Everything he didn't want to know but needed to.

Nina felt free. Ry didn't look at her has if she needed mental help. He listened intently and read H. Anderson's letter as if it were the most important thing in his world. He seemed to understand fully the mixture of fear and emotions that had taken up residence inside her since she had begun her journey.

He seemed truly concerned for her welfare, and that amazed her. A few days ago, she would never have believed it, but it was as if they were meant to be. Now, as she sat beside him on the couch watching him read the letter again, she chastised herself for such foolish thoughts.

He folded the letter and handed it to her—glanced at the photo of her father and the other two men, but didn't touch it. Just left it lying on the table in front of them.

When she looked into his eyes, something distant lingered there—a sadness she didn't understand. He gave her a smile laced with sorrow.

"What's wrong?" she asked. Dread filled her. He had been supportive a minute ago, but now he looked as if he might collapse. She didn't understand.

"What do you think of this H. Anderson?" He motioned toward the letter that now lay in her lap.

She glanced down at it. "What do you mean, 'what do I think'?"

"Do you think he's telling the truth? What makes you think he's telling the truth?"

She shrugged. "It never really occurred to me that he might be lying. Why would he lie? And what about the H. Anderson that just killed himself? And what about the fire at the Lamplighter? Is it all coincidence or should I be scared, Ry? Because, I'm scared. I'm really scared."

Without hesitation, he pulled her into his arms. She could feel his heart beating against her temple, could hear it syncopating a rhythm with the pulse in her ears. She closed her eyes.

"Don't be scared," he murmured against her hair. And all her fear vanished.

He squeezed her tighter, and warm security enveloped her. She had been right to trust him.

Chapter Nine

Sheriff Harper was busy cleaning his revolver when Ry walked through the door to the police station. Harper briefly looked up before returning his attention to the job at hand. He then, evidently, had a second thought. He put the gun on his desk and stood. "Andies, we need to talk."

Ry flopped into one of the chairs and put his feet up on the desk, waiting for Harper to open his mouth.

Harper perched on the corner of the same desk, his wide buttocks squeaking across the wood, the legs—his and the desk's—crackling under the weighty frame. "We need to come to some kind of understanding, me and you."

"What kind of understanding?"

"Well, Tony's my brother-in-law . . ." Harper wagged a finger at Ry, and Ry contemplated snapping it off at the knuckle. As if Harper had read Ry's mind, he snatched his hand back. "Look, Tony's kin, and we need to keep a good relationship me and him, and you've been screwing it up."

"What can I do about it?"

"You could put in a good word for me every now and then.

He seems to respect your opinion. He trusts you, and if you trusted me then maybe he would too. As it is, he treats me like a moron."

Ry held back the urge to tell Harper that he was a moron. "He treats everyone like a moron. It's his job. He's the boss."

"Yeah, but . . ."

"All right." Ry put his palm up. "I'll see what I can do, but I can't make any promises."

"Yeah, sure." Harper nodded and slid his overweight posterior off the desk. "I'm sure you'll do your best. It's not *your* wife breathing down your neck to get in tight with her rich brother." He moped all the way back to his desk and resumed cleaning his gun.

"Why'd she marry you in the first place?" He shouldn't have asked. He really didn't care. The question just slipped out before he could stop it.

"None of your business!" Harper said waving the gun at Ry. "She loves me. Is that so hard to believe?" He shook his head and put down the gun. "Just don't start with me. I get enough grief from Tony without you jumping on me too."

"Geez," Ry said, getting up. "We a little touchy this afternoon or what?" He walked to the back room and opened a file cabinet. He wasn't really looking for anything new, he just needed to look for something to tell Nina—something that would be both satisfying and final. He needed to douse her curiosity before she decided to take matters into her own hands—a lethal decision for both of them, Ry was sure.

He pulled out the drawer and then glanced back at the sheriff. Harper's mealy mouthed groveling left a bad taste in Ry's mouth. The man had always been a weasel, but he had never asked for Ry's help before. In fact, his usual mode was trying to build himself up while knocking Ry to the ground.

Something was up, and Ry didn't like it.

*   *   *

Nina finished eating an egg salad sandwich and then covered the leftovers with plastic wrap. Ry had been gone all morning, and she was getting more and more agitated as the day wore on. She'd wasted a whole afternoon by taking his advice, and now he hadn't shown up with any information.

He said he would help. He said she should take it easy. *Take it easy.* How could she? He hadn't so much as called. What could be so difficult about finding the information she wanted? Harvey Orwell at the Lamplighter had known immediately about the accident when she'd mentioned it, so there couldn't be many fatal accident reports in the police files. *There's something fishy going on,* she grumbled silently. *I'm going to talk to Wilbur Chase.* He knew more than he had put in the article. She was sure of it.

Nina put the egg salad in the refrigerator, then finished the glass of water she had on the counter. Her thoughts never left Wilbur Chase. She should have stayed outside his door the other day and forced him to talk somehow, but she'd been so startled by his response she hadn't known how to react. Today, she would have more resolve. Today, he wouldn't scare her away. *Please, God, don't let him scare me away.*

She jotted a note about the egg salad being in the refrigerator then grabbed her purse and ran out the door.

The apartment was empty when Ry got home. A combination of dread and relief washed over him. He wondered where Nina was, but he'd spent all morning trying to figure out what half-truths to tell her, and he hadn't thought of any. Her absence bought him a little more time.

A note on the kitchen table told him there was fresh egg salad in the refrigerator. He hated egg salad. Instead, he nuked a hot dog in the microwave and fed the garbage disposal two tablespoons of egg salad. Nina had been nice enough to fix him lunch. He didn't want to insult her by not eating any of it.

She really was a great woman, when he had time to think about it. Lately, he'd been thinking about it too much. He needed to be thinking about closing this case. It had taken him years to get this far. He couldn't let one curious woman ruin everything—even if the woman was Nina Thomas. He pushed aside the memory of what had happened between them last night. He'd been a fool, but he hadn't been able to stop himself. If it weren't for their current situation, he wouldn't mind. As it was, he needed to keep his distance.

What would she do if she found out who H. Anderson actually was? Ry could never let her find out. If she did, she'd hate him for sure.

And hate certainly wasn't what he wanted her to feel for him. God help him, all he really wanted was her back in his arms.

Where was she, anyway? He stuffed the last bit of hot dog bun into his mouth and decided to check in.

He was about to pick up the phone when it rang.

"Yeah?"

"Ry, we need to talk, me and you."

"Mr. Carlucci? That you?"

"Yeah, it's me, and I ain't happy."

"What's up?"

"I want you to come down here right now."

"To Texas?"

"Of course to Texas, stupid. You're on the next flight out of Flag."

"Okay, Mr. Carlucci. I'll be there."

Ry disconnected then dialed D.C. Beads of sweat formed on his brow as he listened to Lottawalski's phone ringing.

"Lottawalski."

"It's me. I think we may have a problem," Ry said.

"Why do you always call me when we have a problem? Why can't you call and tell me that you've got Carlucci in custody with air-tight evidence and a sure conviction?"

"Carlucci just called me. He wants me in El Paso, pronto. Check the wire."

"What for?"

"If I knew what for I wouldn't be calling you, would I? He just called—which in itself spells trouble because he never personally calls anyone. I'm supposed to be on the next flight out of Flagstaff."

"Well, you have to go, of course," Lottawalski said.

"Thanks."

"What I mean is, you can't *not* go. I'll just have to alert the El Paso office and make sure there's a lot of back-up around if you need it."

"Well, Lance. If I don't see you again, it's been nice knowing you."

"Give me a break, Anderson. We'll be golfing in no time." He paused and then added, "Good luck, buddy."

"Thanks. I think I'm going to need it. You know what it means for somebody to get called out."

"You'll be fine," Lottawalski assured Ry.

But he didn't sound too sure.

Nina took a deep breath before getting out of her car. If her last encounter with Wilbur Chase was any indication, getting him to open the front door was going to take a lot of doing. She made her way up the narrow walk to Wilbur Chase's front door and rang the bell. No answer. She rang again, then banged on the door. "Please, Mr. Chase. I really need to speak to you."

From inside she could hear the faint sound of wheels on wood, and then the familiar face appeared at the window.

"Go away, child. I have nothing to say to you."

She stepped on the grass to peer at Wilbur Chase through the window. "Please, Mr. Chase. I need some answers. What are you afraid of?"

"I—I'm not afraid of anything, you sassy cuss. Now get off my property before I call the . . . before I get my shotgun."

He started to back his wheelchair away from the window, and Nina yelled, "I'm staying until you open the door. I'll ring your doorbell continuously." He kept backing away, so she yelled louder, "You won't get rid of me, Mr. Chase! Not unless you open the door."

He paid no attention to Nina's threats, just disappeared from view.

Nina sat on the porch step and looked at her watch. When a couple of minutes had passed, she stood and rang the doorbell a few dozen times. Still the old man would not answer the door. She waited a few more minutes, then rang the bell again. Still, the door did not open.

After two hours of ringing the doorbell every few minutes, Nina began to believe she was wasting her time. Wilbur Chase was obviously not going to answer the door, and sitting on his porch accomplished nothing but increasing her frustration. Nina plopped onto the step, hiding her face in her hands. Why wouldn't anyone cooperate? The need to give up and go back to Colorado was almost overwhelming, but she couldn't give up. Unbidden, the tears spilled over her eyelids.

"Now don't go and do that. If I'd known you was gonna weep all those tears, I'd have let you in ages ago."

Shocked at the sound of the old man's voice, Nina shot up and jerked around. "You mean you're going to talk to me?"

"Might as well. My life's done for anyhow," he said. Regardless of his nonchalant tone, he nervously peered down the street before raising a shaky hand to wave Nina inside. She followed his gaze down the road but didn't see anything of note. She turned back to him and gave him a smile.

With new optimism blossoming inside her, Nina entered the old house. It smelled musty despite the fact that it looked clean enough.

"I really appreciate this," Nina said, going to the rickety ladder-back chair Wilbur Chase offered. She eased into it, and it creaked in protest. She gently shifted her weight.

"Sorry I don't have anything better for you to sit on. Being in this chair and all, I don't have much use for furniture these days."

"Oh, it's all right," Nina said as she scanned the dreary living room.

It was dim, the front window adding hardly any light. The area rug, an ancient braided oval in beige and chocolate brown, matched the color of the curtains, and as far as furniture went, the room was sparse. Besides the chair on which Nina sat, there was a stool and a small table that housed the television.

Nina turned her attention back to the old newspaper man and smiled. "I can't say enough how much this means to me."

"Before you go blowing thanks around, don't you think you ought to see if I'm even gonna be of help?"

"Yes . . . well . . . I—I guess." Nina crossed one leg over the other. The chair groaned, and she quickly uncrossed her legs. "I really would like to know all I can about the accident that happened. You know, the one I mentioned the last time I was here?"

"Yes, I know the one. It's the only car accident that's killed anyone since."

"You're kidding. There hasn't been one fatal accident here in fifteen years?" Nina was astonished. If that were the case, why hadn't Ry been able to tell her anything?

A seed of doubt about him sprouted a little root.

"Nope. Not a one. Been some pretty serious wrecks, mind you, but nobody's ended up dead."

"Well, in that case, Mr. Chase . . ."

"Wilbur," he corrected.

Nina smiled. "Wilbur," she conceded. "In that case, Wilbur, why is it so difficult for me to get any information about it?"

"How am I supposed to know? I was told to leave it alone. I was told I'd wind up with my a—backside—in a sling if I didn't forget about the whole thing." The tremoring of his head worsened Nina noticed, but she had to get to the truth.

"But why?"

"Well, I didn't think old Pete would have been doing anything to wind up dead. See, I kind of took a liking to him—"

"You knew him?" Nina interrupted.

"You going to let me tell the story or what?"

"Sorry."

"Now where was I?" He put a thoughtful finger to his temple. "Oh, yeah, I remember. Well, I took a liking to him for several reasons. One, he was a vet. Vietnam, you know. Two, he loved his little girl so much he'd have done anything for her. In fact, I still ain't so sure he wasn't doing just that when he got killed." He looked at her thoughtfully. "You know, you kind of look like her a bit."

Nina cringed. "You mean it's because of his daughter that he's dead?"

"Of course not. She was just a kid—eight, nine, something like that. What I mean is, I think something underhanded was going on, and he stumbled upon it and had to take off to save his kid's hide. That's what I meant."

"In other words, if he hadn't had is daughter to look after, he might not have fled and may still be alive today. So, in a roundabout way, it is her fault," Nina concluded.

Wilbur let out a wheezy hiss. "What the heck's wrong with you twisted people today? There ain't no way a kid could be responsible for anything, so quit trying to make a story where there ain't one." He shook his head. "If it ain't tabloid juicy, nobody wants it. Shame. Real shame."

"Story? You think I'm a reporter?" Nina asked incredulously.

"Ain'tcha?"

"No. No, I'm not."

Wilbur shrugged. "You know about old Sheriff Harper, right? He hasn't got a brain cell in his whole head. Nobody around here likes him. He's an idiot. Well, some weird things were happening right before Pete died. Two deputies disappeared . . ."

"What do you mean they disappeared?"

"Just what I said; they disappeared. Harper said they moved out of state, but I don't trust him as far as I could throw him—which ain't far these days. Anyhow, nobody thought anything about it at first. Mostly, nobody thought anything about it ever. But me being nosy and all, I kept tabs. Anyway, it was about that time that this other deputy . . . what was his name? Oh, I can't remember. Anyway, *he* was kicked off the force. It was never fully let out about why, just something to do with drugs. That's when I started getting suspicious about the other two disappearing." He stopped and looked thoughtful for a moment and Nina almost said something, but he turned back to her and resumed his story.

"About that time, old Pete ended up dead, and me being the cynical mind I am put two and two together and smelled a dead fish. Know what I mean?"

Nina nodded even though she really didn't. She just wanted Wilbur to keep talking.

"I found out that Harvey . . . that was his name! Harvey Something—I don't remember his last name. Anyway, Harvey was the guy that got kicked off the force. I found out that he and Pete had known each other in Vietnam. I know that's not a big thing, since everybody and their brother was over there fighting a war they didn't want to be in, just so they could come back and get spit on . . ."

Nina raised an eyebrow.

"Sorry. I get carried away sometimes. It just really gets my goat about those poor vets, and all. I know what it's like to go fight in a war. It's hell is what it is. 'Course, I had a nifty home-coming, not anything like those 'Nam vets. Anyway, I found out they'd known each other, and I'd started doing some more digging when Sheriff Harper comes up to me one day and says, 'Watch your back if you keep digging. You best just keep your nose on your face and out of other peoples' affairs.' That's what he told me."

"Why didn't you keep digging anyway?" Nina asked.

" 'Cause I like my nose on my face, that's why."

"But how could you? A great injustice might have been happening underneath your very nose, and you could've had the power to stop it."

"Who do I look like, Clark Kent? Bullets don't bounce off my chest, and Harper doesn't hand out idle threats neither. He may be a small town yokel, and he may be a pain sometimes, and he may even be a little ignorant, but when he says watch your back, he means watch your back."

She eyed him seriously. "I don't believe that's all that happened. I've read your articles. You were an investigative reporter. You had passion. Valued the truth. It's evident in your writing. One threat wouldn't have frightened you away. Tell me what else happened."

His gaze darted around the room as if he thought they could be overheard sitting in his living room. He let out a long breath. "Nah, I didn't quit, and one night I stumbled upon Harper and his brother-in-law counting a briefcase full of money. I don't know how much it was, or where it came from, but they beat me pretty good. One of my kidneys collapsed, broke my back in three places—crippled me for life."

Nina was stunned. What had she walked into? "But . . . why didn't you report them?"

"To who? The sheriff?" He shook his head. "Nobody would have believed me. Harper's an upstanding citizen. I was just a troublemaker."

"Well, what about now?"

"Now I'm a broken, useless old man. Everybody knows it, and I want to keep it that way.

Ry paced the floor. His packed bag lay at the door. He was ready to walk out, but thoughts of Nina stopped him. If he was in Texas, Nina would be alone. Or, to be more precise, would be left to the wiles of Sheriff Harper. Ry shuddered at the thought. He looked at his watch, not really seeing what time the hands read. *Where is she?* He wanted her back before he left. He wanted to make sure she wouldn't do anything until he got back—if he got back.

He pushed that thought out of his mind and forced himself to sit down. After a few seconds, he was back on his feet, too antsy to sit still. He picked up the phone, ready to call Lottawalski but reconsidered and put it back down. Finally, he just jotted a note, grabbed his suitcase, and ran out the door.

Nina left Wilbur Chase's house frazzled and confused. The more she discovered, the less she understood. The less she understood, the more frightened she became. She had gotten more than she'd bargained for when she began her journey. Drugs, disappearing cops, threats from the sheriff. As she sat in her car and thought about it now, she wasn't sure what she'd expected. She was investigating an accident that had suddenly become murder with the arrival of a letter. What *had* she expected? Certainly not anything as complex as this. She didn't know what to think. Didn't know what to do. Maybe Ry would be able to help her. She was grateful she had someone she could trust. Someone who would help her get to the truth in all this.

A smile curved her lips as she thought of him. She could still feel his arms around her—strong, protective, caring. A shield she could carry with her. So many years she had been unwilling to confide her past, her fears to anyone. But last night she had confided everything to Ry, and he had embraced her, not pushed her away. She had even told him about the rash of child psychologists, her nightmares while growing up, and the block in her memory. He knew everything there was to know about her, and he hadn't reacted as if she had two heads. If anything, he had done the opposite. Nothing came as a shock to him. Nothing.

He'd held her in his arms and assured her that everything would be okay. That he would see to it. That she could trust him. And she did.

She arrived at the apartment and half-expected him to be waiting for her, but he wasn't. The only thing she found was a note on the refrigerator, obviously scribbled quickly by the look of the untidy handwriting. It said: *Away on business. Don't know when I'll be back, but make yourself at home. Ry.*

A strange, empty feeling closeted Nina as she read the note. She was alone—all alone. But why should that bother her? Until the fire had obliterated her belongings she'd been alone and hadn't thought anything of it. Now, after a few days with Ry, she felt desolate without him.

She sank onto the sofa and tried to put the puzzle pieces together in her head. Dirty cops. Drug deals. Threatened reporters. Mysterious disappearances and an accident that wasn't an accident. Sounded like something out of a movie. Her head began to hurt. She took an aspirin out of her purse and swallowed it without water. Propping her head on the arm of the sofa, she closed her eyes and willed her mind to go blank.

It almost worked.

Chapter Ten

Ry almost got run over by a forklift as he entered the warehouse in El Paso. The driver shouted a profanity at him, but Ry didn't respond. His nerves were shot. He knew there was trouble if Carlucci had personally summoned him here.

Every fiber of his being was electrified as he scanned the rows of crates. The heady scent of plywood and glue bit his nostrils, and he snorted. It always felt like sawdust was crawling up his nose when he walked through here. He hated it.

Rounding the last row, he looked up the flight of metal stairs and into the glass-encased office where he knew Carlucci was waiting. The thought sobered him quickly. He might enter that office alive but exit on a stretcher. Adrenaline shot through his body, and his pulse battered his temples. He swallowed hard as he climbed the stairwell, sure that his heartbeat was loud enough to be heard by others. He'd barely reached the landing when the office door flew open.

"Ry! I thought you'd never get here. Come in, come in." Carlucci put a friendly hand on Ry's back and gave him a fatherly pat. The pungent Italian cologne that was the man's aroma of choice wafted up Ry's nose and mingled with the plywood and glue smell that still lingered there. He stifled a sneeze and gave Carlucci what he hoped was a dispassionate smile.

"Sit, sit." Carlucci perched on the corner of a metal desk. "They told me your flight was delayed. Sorry about that."

"It wasn't too bad." Ry studied Carlucci with a wary eye. Nothing seemed out of place. Not the man, not his clothes, not his polished Italian shoes.

That wasn't a good thing.

"Good, good." He nodded, got up, and walked behind the desk to sit down. "I guess you want to know why you're here."

"Well, yes, Mr. Carlucci. I was kind of curious. Is something wrong?" Ry's voice sounded tinny to his own ears. He only hoped it came across as normal to the man sitting opposite him.

"I hope not, Ry. I hope not."

"What do—"

"You see, Ry, this Thomas chick is really getting on my nerves. I guess Harper told you about the stunt at the hotel?" Ry nodded, and Carlucci continued. "Well, he screwed it up again. As you know, the wench wasn't there when he torched the place."

Ry's blood chilled. "You want to kill her? But I thought . . ."

"Don't interrupt, Ry. It really irritates me." The hostile glint in Carlucci's eyes sent a shiver of disquiet scurrying down Ry's back.

"Sorry." He slumped back.

"I can't chance her. We're getting ready to retrieve that Nogales shipment. We've got the biggest transaction in our history about to happen in Baja, and I just can't take any chances. She's got to go."

"But, Mr. Carlucci, she's harmless. I've been watching her every second. She knows absolutely nothing."

"Yeah, I heard you've been watching her. I don't like it, Ry. I don't like that she's at your place. She could find something out. She could go to the Feds. She makes *you* look suspicious."

The assertion was just as much a question as a statement—maybe more so. Ry had to measure his own reaction carefully. "Well, I have to act like the caring deputy when she's around, don't I, boss? If I don't, she won't tell me anything. How else am I supposed to know exactly what she knows? You told me to keep an eye on her, keep you informed. That's what I'm doing. Besides, she doesn't know anything."

"You do have a point, Ry. You do. But look at it from my point of view. I can't take any chances. I've already had one rollover agent almost bring me down."

"Th-that's what you think? That I'm DEA or something?" He laughed as if the idea were absurd. "I hate cops!" Sweat pooled in Ry's armpits, and he felt sticky. The urge to fidget was almost overwhelming, but he kept his head and consciously schooled his expression.

"I'm not saying anything right now. All I know is that we'll know one way or the other within the week."

"What do you mean?"

"You'll have done your job in Nogales and . . ." Carlucci paused dramatically, and Ry's adrenaline pumped a little faster. Carlucci got up and came to stand directly in front of Ry. ". . . and you'll have killed Nina Thomas. No cop would do that." He bored Ry with an icy stare. "And I hope for your sake you're clean."

A shot of fear shook Ry down the length of his spine, then came back up and lodged in his throat. He swallowed it and ignored the threat.

"But, boss, there's no reason to kill her." He kept his tone even, apathetic. He couldn't legitimately go to bat for some woman who'd stumbled into trouble, but he had to try something.

Carlucci's expression hardened. "If she's not dead by the time you go to Nogales, I'll kill you both myself. Got it?"

"Yes, Mr. Carlucci."

Nina dozed on the sofa, subconsciously listening to the hum of the refrigerator as it cycled. The fragrance of roses drifted in on a breeze through the open window across the living room. She was exhausted, emotionally and physically, but felt more relaxed than she had in days. Her mind had finally let go of the investigation and had lulled into peace.

The refrigerator motor had just clicked off when the knock on the door came. It startled her. Ry was out of town, and she didn't expect anyone to visit.

Reluctantly, she dragged herself off the couch, crossed the room, and opened the door. Sheriff Harper stared her in the face, and all the apprehension she had experienced earlier came back in spades and made a home at the base of her neck.

"Good day, Sheriff. What can I do for you?"

"I just stopped by to see how you were doing since Ry is away."

"I'm fine. Would you like to come in?"

"No. I was just checking on you is all. I'll be going." He started to turn away and then stopped. "You gonna be going anywhere later?"

"Excuse me?" Nina's emotions balked at the question—it almost sounded like a threat. Or was she just paranoid because of what Wilbur Chase had told her?

"You going anywhere later?"

"Why?"

"I just thought that if you didn't have any plans you might want to join me and my wife for dinner."

Nina wasn't sure what to think. On one hand it seemed like a strange invitation, but on the other, perhaps it was just small town hospitality. Either way, she wanted to stay away from him. "Thank you, Sheriff. I don't have any plans, but I'd just as soon stay in and relax, if you don't mind. It's been a rough couple of days for me."

"I suppose it has," he muttered before turning his back on her and strolling away.

She closed the door and leaned against it for several seconds before making her way to the kitchen to get something to wash down the touch of misgiving still wedged in her throat.

The phone rang, and she started. Since she knew the call wouldn't be for her, she ignored the ring and poured herself a glass of orange juice. While she drank, she heard the answering machine pick up, but it didn't sound like anyone left a message.

As she entered the living room and got closer to the machine, she heard a distant and muffled, ". . . already killed her . . ." *Click.*

An icy unknown chilled her veins, and she collapsed into the chair by the bookcase. Were they talking about her? Were they talking about Ry?

She thought she could trust him. Now, she wasn't so sure.

Rain beat against the car, making it stuffy and humid inside. Ry felt as if he might smother to death. He opened the phone and dialed a secure channel.

"Lancelot . . ."

"Hey, Rylan, good to hear your voice. How's things in El Paso?"

"Bad, Lance, real bad. We've got us one heckuva of a problem."

"What is it?"

"He wants me to kill her."

"He wants you to what?"

"That's right," Ry confirmed. "He wants her dead by the time we hit Nogales, and he wants *me* to do it."

"I thought you said that he understood she's harmless."

"That's what I thought. But someone's been filling his head with hype, and I can just bet who."

"Harper." Lottawalski sighed. "So what do you propose to do?"

"I don't know. He says that this is the only way I can prove I'm not an agent . . ."

"He knows you're FBI?"

"No, he doesn't know. He's just taking precautions because I've got her staying at the house."

"I told you that was a stupid idea. You should always stick to procedure, Ry. You've been doing this long enough to know that."

Ry ignored the chastisement. Yes, he knew all about procedure, but there was nothing procedural in the way he felt about Nina. "Look, I'll think of something, okay. I'll think of something."

"You don't sound too convinced."

"I will, Lance. I promise I won't let anything happen to her—even if it kills me."

"Yeah, that's what I'm afraid of."

Wilbur Chase sat sleeping in his wheelchair. The television blared a commercial he was oblivious to in his slumber. Behind him, standing in the entryway, Sheriff Harper watched.

He stood silently, listening to Wilbur snore. He didn't know what the big deal was about the old geezer. The man was confined to a wheelchair and never left the house. In fact, Harper couldn't even remember the last time he had seen old Wilbur out and about. It was Wilbur Junior who kept Senior in food and clothes. Still, Carlucci wanted the old buzzard roughed up, and Harper had to do what he was told.

If he played his cards right, he'd end up one wealthy sheriff some day. Carlucci didn't have any heirs of his own, and Harper knew it was only a matter of time before the man left his fortune to his sister.

When Harper had married Irene, he hadn't known about Carlucci. He'd married for love just like all the other schmoes in town. But over the years, Irene had turned into a real witch, and now all he wanted was the money. The trick, though, was doing what he was told and out-living good ol' bro'-in-law, Tony. But Harper was determined.

Smiling, he crept up to the wheelchair and ran a cool finger across Wilbur's balding head. The old man snorted a couple of times, moved his head, and then resumed his steady rhythmic snoring.

Frustrated, Harper shoved a hand into Wilbur's shoulder, making the old man jerk forward in the wheelchair. With a sputtering choke, Wilbur woke up.

"Wh—what is it?"

"It's me, old man," Harper said, spinning the wheelchair around so Wilbur faced him. "What have you been up to?"

"N—not much, Sheriff. What do you want?" Wilbur's head tremored more from fright than from Parkinson's Disease, Harper could tell.

"I want you to keep your trap shut. Got it?" Harper tweaked the old man's nose.

"I don't know what you're talking about, Sheriff. I ain't got much to say to anybody these days."

"That better be the truth, old man, or you're gonna find yourself in a heap of trouble. You get my meaning here?"

"I do, Sheriff. I do. But I'm just an old man minding my own business. You ain't got to worry about me."

"I hope so, Wilbur. I hope so. I wouldn't want to have to help Junior carry your coffin any time soon."

"You threatening me, Sheriff?"

"You know the sheriff doesn't go around threatening good

law-abiding folks like yourself. Let's just call it a warning. Right?"

"Right, Sheriff. Right. I know you're a good man, Sheriff. I do."

"Right, then. I'll leave you in one piece—I mean, in peace. Say 'hey' to Junior when he drops by."

"Okay, Sheriff."

Harper pulled up to the police station with a weathered frown on his face. Most of the things he had to do didn't bother him too much. Most of the people he had to put the pressure on were low-life scumbags who made their living leeching off someone else's bad habits. He didn't mind roughing them up, but Wilbur Chase was a helpless old man, and Harper didn't like the prospect of having to hurt him.

It wasn't really that his ethics got in the way. Ethics didn't enter into it. He'd always been an "every man for himself" sort of guy. He wasn't sure what it was. He only knew that if Tony ordered him to hurt Wilbur bad it was going to be tough—a lot more exacting than having to get rid of Marsh and that other undercover DEA agent. That hadn't been difficult at all. In fact, Harper had rather enjoyed ordering their demise. They'd been traitors—the blatant enemy.

It hadn't been difficult to get rid of Andecof, either, once he started acting strange. Those things were easy, but Wilbur would be a different story. If Carlucci ever found out about Harper's reservations, he'd call him an old fool, soft and unreliable. Harper couldn't allow that, so he would do whatever he was told until the time of his emancipation.

He strolled into the office and found Martinelli perusing the pages of the latest *Sports Illustrated* Swimsuit Edition. "Anything good?" Harper inquired.

"I haven't read the articles yet," Martinelli told him without looking up from the magazine.

"I wasn't talking about the articles, stupid." Harper walked over and poured himself a cup of coffee. Sipping, he asked, "Tony called?"

"Nope."

"You know what he wanted with Andies?"

"You're related to him, what are you asking me for?" The irritation in Martinelli's voice was distinct.

"All right. Finish the stupid magazine. It's as close as you'll ever come to a good-looking woman anyway." Harper slammed his cup on the desk, causing some of the liquid to slosh out, then he headed for the bathroom.

"Look who's talking," Martinelli shot back. "I'm not the one married to the she-devil from hell."

"Screw you," Harper replied as he closed the door behind him. He couldn't be bothered with Martinelli or anyone else for that matter. He needed to figure out a way to keep tabs on Nina Thomas without her getting suspicious. With Andies out of town, he had a real opportunity to impress Tony. And Nina was his first-class ticket to acceptance.

Nina sat cross-legged on the sofa reading *War and Peace*. The television was on, but the volume was muted. The silent figures were there merely as a form of company. She missed Ry. She was afraid. She was afraid of Ry, yet afraid to be away from him. She felt completely incapacitated and fickle. In the past, she'd prided her forthright certainty about everything. Now she found herself wholly unsure. The feeling disconcerted her so much that she'd plunged into the classic novel to keep her mind off other, more dismal, musings. If one thing was certain, it was that she couldn't concentrate on *War and Peace and* other things as well.

She was just about to finish the second chapter when the phone startled her. She dropped the book, losing her page, and snatched up the receiver before it rang again.

"Yes?"

"Miss Thomas?"

Acutely aware that no one should know her whereabouts, Nina was immediately on edge. "Who is this, please?"

"Sheriff Harper, ma'am."

"Oh, Sheriff. What can I do for you?" She relaxed a little, but only a little.

"How are you, Miss Thomas?"

"Well, I'm fine, Sheriff. I thought I told you that earlier."

"Oh . . . yes . . . right . . . well, I just wanted to make sure . . . uh . . . and to extend the invitation to dinner . . . uh . . . just in case you, uh, changed your mind or got lonely or something."

He paused and static stretched across the wire. Nina didn't know what to say, and then Harper's voice broke the silence.

"Well, actually, Miss Thomas, I called to insist you come to our house for dinner. My wife won't take no for an answer. And you know my wife can be real stubborn. Arguing with her when her mind is made up is pretty well useless, if you know what I mean."

"That's very kind—"

"Please, Miss Thomas."

Sheriff Harper made Nina's skin crawl, but she decided the smart thing to do would be to accept his offer. If this man had had anything to do with her father's death, she needed to find out, and the only way to do that was to lay aside her fears and plunge straight into the investigation.

"All right, Sheriff. But call me Nina. How will I get to your house?"

"I'll pick you up in about half hour."

She hung up the phone, found the page she had been reading before the phone had sent *War and Peace* sailing to the carpet, and dog-eared the page. As she stood up, something crunched underfoot. Shifting her foot out of the way, she found a crumpled note. She hoped it wasn't important. Picking it up and smoothing it out with an open palm, she found it was a torn piece of police letterhead. It read: *Wed Tony Nogales 2nd house 500 key deposit.* Who was Tony Nogales? Dismissing the note, she folded it neatly and placed it in her purse. It must've fallen out of the book, but if she put it back in the wrong place, Ry might never be able to find it. She'd keep it where it was least likely to disappear and give it to him when he returned.

Realizing she was running out of time, she rushed to get ready for the sheriff's arrival. She had just stepped back into her shoes when the doorbell rang.

"Ready?" He asked the moment the door opened.

"Sure. Just let me grab my purse." She picked up her shoulder bag then let Sheriff Harper lead her to his patrol car. As she slipped into the passenger seat, the radio transmitted.

"Hey, Harper. You there?"

The sheriff quickly rounded the front of the vehicle and grabbed the microphone through the open driver's door. "Yeah, I'm here. What do you want, Martinelli?" He maneuvered into the seat and turned the ignition switch with his free hand.

"Message from Tony."

"Uh . . . well, I . . . uh, I can't take it right now. I'm busy," he stammered back into the mike.

"Well, you'd better find time!"

"Look, I told you I was taking the Thomas—I mean *Miss Thomas*—home to dinner. How many times I have to tell you not to bother me when I'm off duty—especially when I'm entertaining guests? Got it?"

"Oh, yeah. Right. Sorry. Give me a call when you're free—later tonight. Okay?"

"Yeah."

Nina scrutinized Sheriff Harper. He seemed so weak. She tried to picture him being so tough that he could beat up Wilbur Chase. She shook her head slightly. Sheriff Harper didn't seem like much of a bully to her. Creepy, yes. Bully, no.

He turned and smiled at her.

"It must be terribly frustrating having to be on call all the time."

"Huh? Oh, yeah, it's a real pain. Never get a minute's peace." He looked at her almost expectantly, but she didn't really have anything else to say.

He exhaled. "Ready?" His voice was cheerful now and unwavering.

"As I'll ever be." Nina smiled again, and Harper smiled back before pulling onto the thoroughfare.

Definitely creepy, Nina thought.

They rode in silence, for which she was thankful, until he pulled onto a long, winding driveway and pulled up beside a mansion. She'd expected a modest country house and instead was ushered into a huge colonial replica.

"Nice, huh?" The sheriff asked as they drove up the driveway. "Not what you expected?"

"Uh, yes. It is very nice."

"The wife insisted. Said she liked all them plantation houses in the old Civil War type movies. I could have done without the rigmarole, myself."

Mrs. Harper—Irene, as Sheriff Harper introduced her—was about as incongruent as incongruencies could be. From the picture Sheriff Harper—or Billy Ray, as he told Nina to address him—had painted of the woman, Nina expected her to be an overbearing, large person, perhaps with a deep, resounding, raspy voice. Instead, she was a dainty woman, inches shorter than Nina's five-five, and at least a full foot shorter than her husband. Her long hair was arranged conservatively in a secure chignon and her tiny frame was well covered by a white eyelet cotton blouse, complete with a high collar that framed her face with a lacy fringe. Her flowing floor-length black skirt seemed centuries out of date. But, the monumental surprise came when she spoke. Her voice was melodic and sweet, and Nina could hear the faint hint of an Italian accent. She took Nina's outstretched hand and shook it gently—the kind of handshake that makes liberated businesswomen ill.

"So glad to have you in our home," Irene told her sweetly.

"Thank you for the invitation. You have a lovely home." Nina looked around the expansive foyer. The sheer of white marble floor reflected a coat-rack and an antique settee decorated in rich golden brocade. The house was quite lovely, and Nina thought absently that county policemen must get paid pretty well these days.

After a few generalities, Sheriff Harper—Billy Ray— excused himself, saying that he had to change out of his uniform. Irene escorted Nina into the dining room where a beautifully decorated oblong table was already set with china and crystal. The highly polished mahogany reflected the light from the ornate chandelier that hung from the ceiling in the perfect center of the room.

"I hope you didn't go to all this trouble on my account," Nina offered.

"Oh, no. Billy and I always eat on china. I won't have it any other way. In my family, eating is a luxury to be enjoyed. We Italians love our food, you know. In fact, my brother, Tony, is always telling me I'm too thin for an Italian of forty."

Nina wanted to tell her that she didn't look as old as forty, but decided such a trite compliment might not sit well with this woman she hardly knew. Instead, she offered, "I don't think you're too thin . . . or too fat," she added quickly, hoping she hadn't put her foot into her mouth too awfully far.

Irene smiled and patted Nina's shoulder. "It's quite all right, dear. I know exactly what you mean."

Nina smiled and relaxed a little.

"Shall we sit?" Irene crossed the room, her heels, hidden beneath her skirt, clicking on the marble floor. "I set this place for you, that way you won't feel too removed from things."

She rested her hand on the back of a chair in the middle of the table, and Nina noticed the woman's perfectly sculptured fingernails—pearly peach lacquer. Real, by the looks of it.

"Would you like a drink before dinner? Some sherry or some white wine, perhaps."

"No, thank you. I think I'll just have some water with dinner." She crossed the room and sat in the high-backed chair Irene had suggested. "Have you lived in Shadow Creek long, Mrs. Harper?"

Mrs. Harper sat at the left end of the table with two chairs separating them. "Fifteen years or so, by now, I'd say—and call me Irene."

Nina nodded. "I wouldn't have guessed that long. You still have a slight accent. Italian, right?"

Irene nodded. "We Carluccis never seem to lose it." She changed the subject easily. "I hope you like ravioli. I make it myself. Cheese, you know."

"Oh, indeed."

Sheriff Harper came into the room, and Nina gazed at his feet wondering how he'd gotten so close without her hearing his footsteps. Rubber-soled shoes.

"You gals all right?" He sat at the other end of the table, also two chairs from Nina.

He was dressed in a plaid shirt, gray polyester, boot-cut slacks, and tennis shoes. *How completely different from his wife,* Nina thought.

"I must check on the meal," Irene said, getting up and disappearing out the door.

"So, how you like Shadow Creek? Lot different than Denver, I'd say!" the sheriff interjected with a chuckle. The hairs on Nina's neck prickled again, and her stomach did a 360-degree roll. Her eyes darted to the sheriff's face.

"How did you know I'm from Colorado?"

Although she wasn't really from Denver, the sheriff had come close enough to pique Nina's interest.

"Oh . . . Uh . . . Mags told me. You know, over at the Lamplighter." He put a thoughtful finger to his chin. "Yeah, I'm sure that's who it was."

"Oh." She silently scolded herself for being so suspicious. She was seeing conspiracy everywhere, and that wasn't good. When she'd left home to begin this expedition, she hadn't been so cynical. Talking to Wilbur Chase had changed all that. Hearing the voice on Ry's answering machine had changed that. And she didn't know if that was good or bad. "Yes," she referred to his original inquiry. "I do like Shadow Creek. It seems to have a very restful lifestyle."

"I hear you're investigating an accident?"

"Yes. One that happened about fifteen years ago."

"Any luck?"

"Not so far, no."

Harper smiled, and Nina's brow creased. He quickly smoothed his expression.

"Too bad. Maybe I can help," he offered briskly.

"That's okay. Deputy Andies has offered his assistance. I wouldn't want to trouble the whole department."

"Oh, yeah, Andies . . ."

Harper mumbled something under his breath, Nina thought, but his voice was muffled by the sound of Irene wheeling in a cart of food. "Hope you're both hungry," she said as she stopped the tray between her husband and Nina. "There's Caesar salad," she went on as she filled Nina's bowl with a mountain of food. "And ravioli, of course. And garlic bread. I hope you like it." She went on to top the sheriff's tableware, then her own. As she sat down, she said to Nina, "I usually pray. Do you mind?"

"Not at all," Nina replied, bowing her head. While Mrs.

Harper offered a prayer aloud, Nina silently added a prayer for her safety and for protection from making the wrong decisions. Confusion seemed to rule her, and although she didn't know much about God, deep down, something inside her knew she would need some divine assistance in getting through this ordeal.

The meal was delicious, as Nina commented several times throughout. Irene took the compliments graciously, but not much else was said until the meal was over. Nina offered to help with the dishes, but Irene declined, saying it wasn't proper for guests to help clean up.

Two hours later, as they were sitting in the den discussing literature that the sheriff seemed not to be fond of, Nina realized that she had been with the couple all evening and hadn't been bored once. She was telling Irene about reading *War and Peace* when she realized she hadn't thought about Ry all evening—well, not much, anyway.

"Yes, Tony read that book a long time ago and recommended it to me. I couldn't really get into it, though," Irene commented.

"Well, Irene, I think it's time to change the subject, don't you, dear?" The sheriff got up and took a cigar from the box on the mantle.

"Must you do that, Billy. Nina may not like that smelly thing. Be considerate of our guest . . . after all, you insisted she come."

Harper replaced the unlit cigar and, with a heavy sigh, returned to his chair. "Sorry, Nina," he said, with the tone and pout of a scolded child.

"Oh, it's all right," Nina offered. "I don't mind a bit." She glanced at the mantel clock. "You know, I really should get back. I've got an early day tomorrow."

The sheriff sat up stiffly. "An early day? But you're on vacation."

"Yes," Nina said, getting to her feet, "but it's a working vacation. I've got to find out about that accident."

"What accident?" Irene asked.

"Oh, just an accident that happened a long time ago," Nina dismissed casually. "You might know of it. I hear it's the only one that's been fatal since."

"You mean that veteran and his daughter? Yes, I know the one. It was . . ."

Nina noticed the shut-up-or-else expression on Sheriff Harper's face at the same time as Irene must have, and the woman did just that—abruptly.

"You were going to say?" Nina pressed, as if she hadn't noticed Harper's warning.

"Nothing. Just that it was tragic."

"Oh." Nina turned to address the sheriff. "May I use your restroom before we go?"

"Sure thing," he replied, getting up. "It's right down the hall there."

Nina found her way to the bathroom and breathed in the fresh floral scent of the electric air freshener. It seemed like every time she relaxed her guard, something strange happened.

"Just go to bed, Irene!" The angry tone of Sheriff Harper's voice filtered through the bathroom door just as Nina was about to leave the room. Instead, she decided to stay hidden. The last place she wanted to find herself was in the middle of a family feud.

"How was I supposed to know it was a secret? You tell me nothing, but expect me to know all!"

"Just stay out of it!"

"So she knows my name. So she knows about the accident. With that information and a butcher knife, she could kill herself! I don't know about you, Billy Ray, you make me crazy sometimes."

Nina heard Irene's footsteps battering the floor and decided to wait a few more minutes before leaving the bathroom. Hopefully she could avoid the confrontation. From the sound of things, she'd heard too much already.

Harper watched his wife storm up the stairs. Her footsteps faded quickly and disappeared behind the slamming of a door. Harper gave the stairwell a wry smile. He wouldn't have to worry about making small talk with her for at least a day and a half. Thank God for small mercies.

He turned his attention to the purse Nina had left on the small marble table in the foyer. He glanced down the hall toward the bathroom, then up the stairwell once again.

Perfect opportunity.

He grabbed the purse and rifled through it as quickly as he could, hoping to find anything that would give him the upper hand over his deputy. He found nothing of consequence except a piece of paper—a piece of paper with his own handwriting on it. *What the devil? . . .*

Just then, Nina threw the bathroom latch. He shoved the paper he'd found back into the bag and threw the purse back onto the table.

"Is it convenient for you to take me home now?" Nina asked.

Harper cursed under his breath. Just a few seconds more and he could've read what he'd found. He wiped his brow with the back of his hand and answered Nina. "Sure."

Chapter Eleven

Shadows loomed overhead as Nina stared up at the ceiling.
She had the bedcovers pulled all the way to her chin, but the
chill in her bones refused to warm. Questions played in her
mind like TV reruns. Fear and doubt insinuated themselves.
She wondered why the Harpers had fought so furiously and if
it had really had anything to do with her or if she was just becoming more and more paranoid. She was engrossed in her
thoughts when the phone rang. Her heart rate skyrocketed.
She leaned over and grabbed the phone out of the cradle.

"Hi, Nina. How's it going?"

"Ry?"

"None other."

"Oh, I'm fine. How's your trip . . . where are you anyway?"
Nina shifted to a sitting position. He sounded so normal. Not
like a killer. But she couldn't let herself forget what she'd
heard. Still, something inside her ached as the memory of his
arms around her flooded her mind. Surely he wouldn't harm
her.

Surely.

"Texas. Be back tomorrow or the day after. Not sure. You're not too bored are you?"

"Don't have time to be," Nina told him.

"What do you mean?"

"Sheriff Harper. He invited me for dinner."

"And you went?" His hostile tone startled her.

"Yes, why? Is something wrong?"

"Of course not."

"Look, I know he's your boss, but—what's the problem?"

"I told you, I don't have a problem. I just called to see if you were okay, and you are, so I guess I'll go."

"Okay. Bye." Nina waited for Ry to hang up. Silence stretched on. "Ry?"

"Yeah?" He sighed.

"Why didn't you hang up?"

"I'm hanging up now," he snapped. Then the phone crackled in her ear before the dial tone buzzed.

More than a little dazed, Nina went to bed, but sleep did not overtake her until the early hours of the morning.

Dawn saw her awakened by the shrill ring of an alarm clock she couldn't remember setting. After groping her way out of bed, she found the annoying thing on the kitchen counter. As Nina entered the kitchen, the clock vibrated itself to the edge of the counter. She made a mad dash for it, but it went clanging to the linoleum before she'd sprinted even halfway across the small room. As she picked up the clock, pushing the button to silence it, the phone rang. The clock went crashing to the floor. She bent and grabbed the clock and ran to the phone. By the time she got to it, it had stopped ringing. Frustrated, she picked up the receiver and slammed it down again for good measure.

She fixed herself a meager breakfast of one slice of whole-wheat toast and then set about her plans for the morning. First thing she had to do was visit Wilbur Chase. He'd been helpful once she'd finally persuaded him to talk, and perhaps he could put her mind at rest about Ry. She longed for him to be the honest, protective person who had held her in his arms not so long ago, and it ripped her apart to think he might be someone else. She reminded herself that she hadn't really heard a conversation on that answering machine—just bits and pieces. Words strung together that didn't necessarily mean what she thought they meant. But that sliver of fear that had wedged its way into her heart pierced a little deeper. After everything, had she chosen to trust the wrong man?

Confusion reigned. Nina didn't know what to think. One minute Ry was a villain, the next a knight. Last night he'd called to see if she was all right.

Or had he called to check up on her for some other reason? She just didn't know what to think.

"All right, Martinelli, what did you want?"

"Tony wants the Thomas woman in El Paso."

"Dead or alive." The thought of getting rid of her really shouldn't thrill him as much as it did, but Harper couldn't help it. Something about her made him squirm. And he never did enjoy squirming.

"Since he said he wanted *her* there and not her *body*, I'm assuming alive.

Harper let out a frustrated sigh and then puffed on his cigar. "What does he want her there for?"

"I don't know. He just told me to tell you to 'mind your own business' and do as he says." Martinelli laughed. "Guess he knew you'd ask why, huh?"

"Oh, shut up!" Harper hung up. Sometimes he got really tired of smart aleck deputies who had more guts than brains. He'd show Martinelli who was boss; he'd have Martinelli get rid of the girl.

* * *

The house on Cherry Orchard Way looked as dismal as the first time Nina had parked in front of it. She only hoped it would be easier to get inside. She strode up the walk, absently listening to the click of her heels on the concrete and thought about how exciting it had been as a child to dress up in her mother's high heels and listen to the click-click as she clumsily made her way across the kitchen floor. That had been before her father had died—when she could still remember. He'd been living in Shadow Creek at the time. At seven years old, she'd watched him leave. Now she knew it had been at her mother's request, but then she'd had no clue. Her only reality: Daddy's leaving. It wasn't long after that her mother had contracted chronic hepatitis and Nina had been shuffled to Shadow Creek to live with her father for an indefinite period of time—ultimately until he died. Blaming her father for having left her initially, she hadn't wanted to go. The trip from Colorado had been a silent one. She'd refused to speak to him at all, and she remembered all the cute things he'd tried in an attempt to lighten the tension between them. Looking back, she envisaged a sorrow in his eyes that she had overlooked at the time.

All this she could recall, but she couldn't remember living in Shadow Creek. Returning hadn't jarred any deep-seated memories. Her life during that time had been completely erased from her mind like offensive language from an edited-for-television movie. It was irritating, and she often found herself straining to regain some of her lost past.

She tapped on the door lightly and, moments later, heard the familiar sound of wheels on wood. The door opened cautiously, and was about to be slammed shut, when Nina shoved her foot over the threshold and used her heel as a doorstop. It wasn't the least painful thing she could've done, but it was effective.

"Go away," Wilbur Chase demanded. "You're gonna get us both killed."

Nina shoved her way into the house and closed the door behind her. "No," she said decisively. "I need to ask you some more questions. Please, Mr. Chase."

The old man shook his head. "I ain't got any more answers. You best mind your own business." He turned the chair away from her and wheeled himself down the hall.

Nina did not give up that easily, and she followed him into a sparse kitchen. The counters were bare of any appliances. No microwave or can-opener, no coffee pot or toaster. Nothing. Nina looked around, speechless for a moment.

"Mr. Chase. I only need to know two things," she said finally.

"Nope," he cut in.

"Mr. Chase, *please.* I just need to know where he lived— you know, Pete and his daughter, and I need you to tell me something about Deputy Ry Andies."

"Nope." He spun the chair to face her. "I already told you I ain't got anything else to say."

"Where did he live?"

"You're a persistent little cuss, aren't you?"

Nina stood her ground, staring with intent at the old man.

He sighed then. "Oh, all right. He lived over yonder in the hills, doing odd jobs and such. And don't ask me nothing about no deputies."

"Mr. Chase, you know I'm staying right here in this very room until you answer me."

"Don't like him myself."

"Why?"

"Too sneaky. Always snooping." He turned away from her again and wheeled himself to the refrigerator. He opened the door and pulled out a can of soda. "Now get! You asked two questions. You got two answers. Now get and don't come back, ever."

Nina sighed and left. At least he'd given her something. Sitting behind the wheel of her convertible, she contemplated what Wilbur had told her. "Over in the hills" could mean almost anywhere, so that wasn't much help. Shadow Creek was surrounded by forestry and hills. And he didn't like Ry—thought he was too sneaky. That didn't help her either.

She opened her purse, pulled out the letter from H. Anderson, and read it a few more times. She'd read it so many times now that parts of it were indelibly etched in her mind. "*. . . I thought that Tony could make my life better. . . .*" Could that be . . .

She drove directly to the police station where she found Sheriff Harper deep in the recesses of *Sports Illustrated*. He sat tipped back in the chair, his feet propped up on the desk with the magazine resting on his protruding belly. When he noticed her come in, he quickly set his chair to rights and smiled brightly.

"Good morning, Miss Thomas. What can I do you for?"

"Nothing much, Sheriff. I was just wondering about your wife's brother." She moved to the counter and propped herself on her elbows.

"What do you mean?" The sheriff's face turned a pasty shade of gray, and her internal antennae squawked. She took a deep breath.

"Well, I haven't seen him around that I know of, and your wife spoke so highly of him. I thought I'd like to meet him."

"Oh, well, he's away on business. He's not in town much." The color rushed back into Harper's face.

"Oh, that's too bad, I suppose. Do you miss him much?"

"To tell you the truth, Miss Thomas, Tony and I don't get on. Why all the questions?" She could hear the strain in his voice and knew he was trying to remain civil. What she didn't know, and what caused her own worry to bound out of control, was why talking about his brother-in-law made the sheriff nervous.

"No reason, Sheriff. I just thought after the wonderful meal your wife prepared . . . well she spoke so highly of him . . .

that, well, I just thought, well, like I said, it would be nice to meet him."

Harper sat back in his chair and smiled. "I suppose we might arrange for you to meet him," he said. "I'll let you know."

Nina's skin crawled up her back. He suddenly looked like the cat who had got the cream, and unease perforated her insides. "Well . . . okay then," she stammered. "I guess I'll let you get back to work."

Nina's head began to pound as she traveled down Main Street. She'd gathered a lot of jumbled information that refused to fit together—not in any way that her amateur detective mind could figure out, anyway.

As she passed the Lamplighter Bed & Breakfast, she noted a construction crew had already started the restoration. The gutted strip of rooms still looked conquered and desolate, the blackened, charred wood splintered and crumbling. Thank goodness she hadn't been there when the fire had broken out.

Pulling into the gravel lot, she momentarily watched the workmen clearing through the rubble before she entered the lobby.

Margaret Orwell stood alone behind the counter looking as homey and friendly as ever.

"Hi, Mags."

"Well, child, I didn't expect to see you. Figured, you'd run along home by now." She smiled warmly.

"I see they've already started fixing up the place." Nina leaned on the counter. "I didn't get to tell you, but I really am sorry about what happened."

"No harm done," Margaret said looking heavenward. "The Lord done taken care of everything." She made eye contact with Nina and smiled angelically. "So what brings y'here?"

"I was just driving by and thought about you. How's Harvey?"

"Fine."

"You've both lived here a long time, haven't you?"

"I bin here all m'life. I remember when Harv strode into town. Must be pert-near forty years ago now. He was the handsomest thing I ever saw. 'Course I was just a youngen then m'self. Didn't know much 'bout boys, y'know. But ol' Harv caught my eye . . ." She smiled wistfully. "We moved away for a time, but we came back. I just couldn't stay away."

"You know almost everyone in Shadow Creek, then, I'd imagine."

"If I don't know 'em, I sure heard enough about 'em. I can tell you that."

"I had dinner with Sheriff Harper and his wife last night. Nice people."

"Yep. I reckon the Harpers some of the nicest people around." She picked up the registration book and began to thumb through it.

"Mrs. Harper told me she's from Italy, or somewhere. She's got an interesting accent. I really enjoyed the evening."

"That's nice, hon'."

"I was trying to remember her maiden name. You wouldn't happen to know what it is?"

Margaret replaced the register and eyed Nina. "W—why don't you ask her yourself. If she already told it to you once, she ain't gonna mind telling you again."

"You're right, Mags . . ." Nina smiled graciously ". . . but, I'd hate to insult her by not remembering, you know. After she's been so nice to me."

"Well, I . . ."

"You will help me, won't you, Mags? I'd hate to insult her and make a fool of myself."

Margaret shrugged. "Well, I don't see's there's any harm, since she's already told you once. It ain't like it's a secret. It's Carlucci."

"That's right. She's got a brother. Tony Carlucci."

Margaret's face lost all color. "I—I really hafta git back to my chores, Nina, b—but I'm glad you stopped by."

"Oh, I'm sorry, Mags. I didn't mean to keep you from work."

Ry lay on the couch, staring at the ceiling. He had to think of a way to manage this mess. Not only had he allowed Harper to get his claws into Nina, he, himself, had been ordered to murder her. He was at a crossroads, and he wanted to travel both directions. On the one hand, he just wanted to run. Take Nina. Get as far away from Carlucci and Harper and all he had seen and experienced in the last few years. On the other hand, he wanted to see this thing finished. See it through 'til the end, not check out because life got a little tough.

The image of Harry's dead body invaded Ry's thoughts. No, he definitely wouldn't check out when things got tough as some people did. He would figure a way to take down Carlucci's operation and save Nina. It wasn't the first time he'd been in a bind. Not the first time he'd been reluctant to stay undercover. It wasn't even the first time his cover had been compromised.

But three years was a long time to assume an identity. And then there was Nina. The way he felt about her was beyond words. He didn't love her, he told himself. Hadn't known her long enough to love her. But she was definitely more important to him than any assignment should be.

The aroma of her hair washed over him, and he closed his eyes to drink it in. He could feel the soft strands tickling his face as if she were actually here with him now. She had felt good in his arms. Like she belonged. Like she wanted to be there. And he wanted to—*Uggh!* He let out a growl. He couldn't even stand the thought of her getting hurt, and that was dangerous—for everybody.

He had to get his head screwed on straight.

He picked up the phone and ordered a pizza, then decided to

take a quick shower while he waited for it to arrive. Maybe if he could keep his mind off everything for a while, he might awaken with a new perspective—one with all the right answers.

Sheriff Harper sat at Ma & Pa's diner sipping coffee and munching on a slice of cheesecake. He didn't know how long he'd been there; long enough to devour a steak sandwich and two or three pots of coffee, he supposed. Preoccupied with Nina Thomas, he was almost oblivious to the movements of people around him. Just as he felt on the verge of a breakthrough, Tony wanted her.

He finished off the cheesecake and pushed away the plate. Ma came over and removed the dirty dish, but Harper hardly noticed. With his fingers cradling his head, he peered into the coffee cup as if all the answers could be found there.

He lifted the cup and finished off the last of his drink. Nina had asked Mags about Carlucci. She'd been talking to Wilbur again. She would have to go.

Rich Willis sat in Lottawalski's office, waiting for his friend to pry himself away from a meeting. Rich had been waiting more than half an hour, and he was starting to get antsy about why Lance had called this spur-of-the-moment meeting. It couldn't be good.

He looked around the practical office and wondered what his life would have been like if he'd decided to join the FBI after the war like Lance had done. He couldn't help thinking that if he'd been a little more mellow after 'Nam—had somehow salvaged a semi-normal existence—perhaps he would still be married and none of this would be happening right now.

The last fight he'd had with Emma—the one she kicked him out over—echoed in his mind so vividly he could still hear every angry word as if it had been spoken this morning. "You're a bully now," she'd told him. "You used to be gentle and caring. Now you're nothing but a washed up soldier. A killing machine with no one to kill."

The words had stung. If only she'd been able to understand what he'd been through. After seeing his friends blown to smithereens. After watching children die—sacrificed by being forced to carry grenades into U.S. camps. It was difficult to be tender. He'd hardened himself, conditioned himself to ignore feelings. He couldn't turn it on and off like a light switch, yet Emma demanded affection.

She demanded attention.

She demanded more than he could give her, more than he had.

He turned abruptly when he heard the door open.

"Hey, Rich. Sorry you had to wait so long," Lance said as he crossed the room and rounded his desk. He eased down onto the chair and eyed Rich seriously.

"Cut to the chase, Lance. I know that look." The pins were pulled on the grenades in Rich's gut as he waited for Lottawalski's news. He supposed he should be used to the turmoil by now, but he wasn't. He leaned forward and rested his forearms on his knees.

"Things are getting a little hairy in Shadow Creek. We're going to have to do something drastic."

"What's that supposed to mean? How 'hairy'? How 'drastic'?"

"Anderson's been ordered to kill Nina." Lottawalski blurted the fact as if his haste might lessen the shock. He was wrong.

"What?" The grenades exploded, leaving Rich's insides empty and hollow. He flew to his feet in one fluid motion, deliberate and lightning-quick.

"Calm down," Lottawalski coaxed, getting to his feet to meet Rich's gaze. "We've got everything under control . . ."

"Doesn't sound like you've got much under control to me." Rich turned away and began to pace the floor. "I'm going."

"No. We can't risk blowing Anderson's cover. We've worked too long and hard to do that."

Rich continued, in silence, to pace the floor, doing nothing else but shake his head.

"Rich, c'mon." Lance moved around the desk and put his hands on Rich's shoulders. "Look at me, buddy. Look me in the eye and tell me you don't trust my judgment . . ."

Rich slowly raised his gaze to Lottawalski.

"Tell me you don't trust that I know how to take care of Nina. You trusted me in Hanoi when I carried you out of that minefield, just like I trusted you years later when you told me you'd seen two small-town policemen shot. I risked my career for you back then, and you know it."

Rich nodded and listened to his friend.

"Nobody wanted to believe those men had been executed. *I* was the one who trusted you. *I* was the one who found out what the DEA was up to, and I was the one who made sure I was on the case when those agents showed up dead. Now all I'm asking you to do is trust me."

Rich shook his head emphatically. "You know I trust you. You know I'd give my life for you. You know it, and I know it. But you're asking me to risk Nina's life, you know that, right? You can't expect me to sit around and do nothing. I've been doing that for too long."

Lance let out a long, slow breath. "You're risking your identity."

"It's not that risky, Lance. Nobody's going to recognize me. I look so different now. Besides, I'll be in and out in a flash." He implored his friend with his gaze. "Please, Lancelot. I've stayed out of it this long. I let you have your way, but now it's time to let me in. Trust me."

Lance gave Rich a sober look. He nodded slowly. "Okay, man. I trust you. You can go."

*   *   *

Carlucci. That was his name. Nina walked into Ry's apartment with more enthusiasm than she'd felt since arriving in Shadow Creek. She had actually done a pretty good job of getting that information out of Margaret Orwell, and now, Nina felt as if she could do anything. Forget Harper and Ry. She would no longer be tentative, scared, or wishy-washy. She would find out what had happened to her father without their help if that's what it took.

She called Ginny, her friend and coworker, and asked her to look up the name Tony Carlucci in Arizona and Texas. Then, not wanting to waste any more time, she decided to check the hills to see if she could find her father's cabin. Perhaps there were still come clues to his death there.

She hadn't gotten far along Main Street when sirens screamed and lights flashed in her rearview mirror. An ambulance and police car whizzed by as she pulled to the side of the road. She swallowed the lump of apprehension that rose to her chest and then followed the sirens. As she trailed them onto Cherry Orchard Way, her heart began to pound against her ribs.

Wilbur Chase.

Nina slammed the stick into neutral and killed the ignition in one fluid motion then bolted from the car. Pushing past a few spectators, Nina rushed into the house. Sheriff Harper was leaning over Wilbur Chase, who lay unconscious on a stretcher. The two paramedics looked annoyed with the sheriff, but remained stiff and silent while the man whispered into their patient's ear.

"Sheriff, what happened?"

Harper straightened at the sound of Nina's voice. "Looks like food pois'nin' or something. Don't know yet." He shook his head sympathetically. "Terrible. Just terrible."

Nina looked at Wilbur. Suspicion hung in her mind like a storm cloud waiting to burst. The old man had been very distant and nervous the last time she'd spoken to him. He'd even warned her to mind her own business. Was it merely coincidence that this accident should befall him now, or was this "accident" as accidental as her father's car crash had been? She eyed Sheriff Harper to see if he looked guilty.

He lifted one corner of his mouth. "This must be hard for you to see, Miss Thomas. Nina. Why don't you let me take you outside?"

She allowed him to guide her through the room and out the front door, still wary even though he looked sincere enough.

"He'll be all right, won't he?" she asked.

"I don't know, to tell you the truth."

Nina paused for a moment, weighing her next move, wondering if she should come right out and ask him—accuse him— of . . . of what? Murdering her father? Poisoning an old man? Was she insane? She had decided just this morning that she was on her own in this. She'd figure it out on her own and then go the police if she had to. And, she'd better speed up her investigation before she too became an "accident" victim. The thought made her shudder.

The misgiving must have been apparent because Sheriff Harper asked, "Are you all right?"

"Ye—yes, thank you, Sheriff." Nina began to move away from him. "I guess I'll be going now. Please let me know if I can do anything for Mr. Chase." She eased her way to the car as if any sudden movements might telegraph her unease.

The sheriff said something, but Nina didn't register what it was. She climbed into her car and fired the ignition without giving the sheriff, or Wilbur Chase's house, another look.

She made her way out of town, and as she entered the serenity of the woods, it was as if all her anxiety melted into nothing. The pavement ended, and she continued her trek along a hard dirt road surrounded by aged, stately evergreens.

Coming to a clearing, she stopped and got out. The fresh air cooled her nostrils as she breathed deeply. It smelled of pine, and she smiled as she thought of how peaceful it would be to live out here away from the hustle and hassles of life.

Taking a walk through the trees, she began to explore. Maybe she could find where she had lived with her father.

After half an hour, she gave up and returned to her car. Not much farther down the path, she came to another clearing.

There, in the midst of fallen, aged pine needles, a small cabin stood weathered and rotted. Through a broken window, a ripped and forsaken curtain rippled in the breeze.

Nina approached cautiously, not really knowing why. The place just seemed a little spectral in its abandonment. She knocked lightly on the door—just in case, although it was obvious that no one had resided there in a while. When nobody answered, she entered.

The cabin consisted of only two rooms. A living room-kitchen combo and a tiny bathroom. The weathered and sparse furnishings consisted of nothing more than a rustic wooden-armed sofa bed.

The kitchen housed a small wet-bar refrigerator that wafted mustiness as Nina opened it. Shaking off the stale stench, she shut the door and investigated the small kitchen area further. The chipped porcelain sink looked as if the tap had dripped into it for eons before the water had finally been disconnected. There was a dent in the sink where the water had staked its claim and eroded the porcelain, and a rust stain draped the side beneath the faucet fixture.

The steel taps were rusted, or maybe it was hard water deposits. Nina couldn't be sure. But the place was a disaster.

Turning to the closet across the room, a single garment caught her attention.

She crossed the room and pulled the small skirt from its

hangar. Blue and green plaid. Her mouth fell open, and a chilly memory skittered down her back. "This is mine," she said aloud. The memory burned, and she dropped the skirt.

Like a strobe light flashing on bits of memory from the past, Nina envisioned herself wearing the skirt. Her father appeared, laughing. They were playing hide-and-seek in the woods. He always let her win, either by making a noise when he hid, or by allowing her to cheat and peek while he found his hiding place. He never found her on time—or almost never. Even though she was old enough to play fairly, he always treated her like a fragile porcelain doll.

He'd always been so happy, except for the day . . . a week before the accident . . . he'd yelled and spanked her for something long forgotten. It had shocked her. It was the only time he'd ever spanked her. If she concentrated hard, she could remember him losing his temper and snapping at her a lot in that final week.

Once, she'd sneaked up on him, and pure reaction had made him almost hit her in the face. He'd yelled at her initially, telling her not to scare people like that, but afterward he had taken her in his lap and rocked her.

"I'm sorry, Nina. I didn't mean to scare you, but you really shouldn't sneak up on me like that."

She pictured herself as a child on his lap. She could hear his soothing voice. Why couldn't she remember more?

Nina heard rustling behind her and turned abruptly. Nothing. She sighed her relief. It was probably just the wind. She shivered just the same.

Deciding to take the skirt, she picked it up and returned to her car. She would go back and call Ginny. Maybe she had been lucky.

Chapter Twelve

Rich Willis sat on the 757 with his tray table locked into an upright position. It had been at least twenty minutes since the flight attendant had informed him—him and everyone else—that he was free to move about he cabin, yet he was as locked into an upright position as that tray table. He would have to get through this flawlessly in order to keep everyone alive. Himself. Nina. Ry. It was a lot of pressure for an aging man. He hadn't had to be completely invisible in years, and he wondered at his own sanity in plunging into this so rashly.

He didn't have a choice, though.

Anxiously, he watched the FASTEN SEAT BELT sign, and after an eternity, it lit. The pilot announced, "We are approaching Sky Harbor Airport. It's sunny and warm in Phoenix. The temperature is one hundred and six degrees. The seat belt sign is lit. Please return your seats to an upright position. Thank you for flying with us. We hope you enjoyed your flight."

If you only knew, Rich thought.

The airplane touched down smoothly, and against instruction,

Rich unbuckled his seat belt. He was on the edge of his seat long before the airplane taxied up to the jetway.

Rich wended through the airport bustle, nothing to worry about but his small carry-on and the weight of the world. He scratched his chin and cheeks. This three-week-old beard was a pain in the back end. He hated beards. Hippies sported beards, and he hadn't been a hippie since the draft had yanked him into hell.

A man sporting a pretty heavy beard of his own pushed past him. Rich grumbled. "Excuse you!" he called out, but the guy didn't seem to notice.

Typical!

Rich reached into the breast pocket of his shirt and pulled out a pack of Camels. He hadn't smoked in years, but lately his nerves had needed the shot of nicotine. It could be worse, he supposed. He could've drunk himself happy and not been any good to anybody. At least this way his mind was still in control—he hoped, anyway.

Lighting the cigarette, he took a long drag. As he walked past the Pizza Hut, the sweet scent of roasting cheese and pepperoni aroused his stomach. He hadn't eaten anything all day, but he wasn't about to stop for a bite now. Hungry or no, he was anxious to get to Shadow Creek. Food could wait until Nina was safe.

God, let Nina be safe.

"Hey, Ginny, it's me. Did you find anything out yet?"

"Not yet, but don't worry, I will. Give me the number, and I'll call you back in a jiffy."

"No! I'm not at . . ."

"I could leave a message . . ."

"No! I'll call you. Don't leave a message anywhere. Do you understand? Not anywhere."

"Okay," Ginny sounded a little startled by Nina's hasty re-

sponse. A pause drew out between them, and Nina felt bad for
snapping at her friend. But she couldn't tell Ginny what she
was doing or anything else that was going on. She couldn't
jeopardize Ginny's safety.

Nina made sure to speak her next words calmly. "Don't leave
a message anywhere, okay? I'll call you. And, Ginny, I really
appreciate your help."

"Nina? Are you okay? You're not in any trouble, are you?"
Ginny sounded truly concerned.

"Not as long as you don't go leaving messages for me. All
right? I'll call *you*."

"I warned him," Harper told Carlucci.

"*Warned* him. I told you to get rid of the old geezer. I didn't
tell you to *warn* him." Carlucci's rage melted the wires con-
necting the phones and scalded Harper's ear.

"He's old, Tony. I poisoned him, for crying out loud. He ain't
gonna talk to nobody for a long time. He ain't even gonna be
out of the hospital before we're done with these big shipments.
You ain't got nothing to worry about."

"You better be positive about that, because if this gets
screwed up, I'm coming after you, kin or no kin. You got it?"

"I got it, Tony. I got it." Harper ran a finger along the inside of
his collar. For some reason the neck seemed to be getting tight.

"What about Ry? He back yet?"

"I don't know, Tony. I ain't seen him."

"You let me know as soon as that Thomas chick's taken
care of."

"Oh . . ." Harper didn't get to finish his sentence before the
dial tone rang in his ear. He slammed down the receiver, and
the phone dinged in protest, but Harper didn't care.

The hour hand crawled around the dial twice while Nina sat
in her car beside the public phone trying to decide what to do

next. She'd found the number to the hospital and called about Wilbur Chase. She was told his condition had stabilized, and he would recover as long as he didn't take a turn for the worse. She felt slightly better, but guilt eroded her insides. He was in the hospital because he had spoken to her. He'd told her as much, and she'd pushed him anyway.

A red pickup pulled up to the mini-mart gas pump, and a man hopped out with a little girl on his heels. Her auburn curls bobbed around her round face. "Daddy, Daddy," she cried as she slipped her hand into his and ran along side him. "Can I have some gum?"

He smiled down at her. "We'll see." He bent down and scooped her up, and she let out a shrill, joyful giggle.

How Nina wished she could remember rides in the car with her father, or going fishing, or buying candy . . . or anything.

Maybe Ginny would have some answers that would bring her closer to revealing the truth. If she couldn't remember what happened, at least she could still discover it.

Nina's fingers trembled as she pushed the buttons on the mini-mart pay phone.

"Nina! You won't believe this guy," Ginny told her excitedly. "He's got import, export businesses from coast to coast. Florida, California, Texas . . ."

"Texas?" The word slapped Nina in the face like a glass of ice water.

"Yeah. Baja, California; El Paso, Texas; Phoenix, Arizona . . . that's not an export company, that's a bottling plant . . . and Nogales, Arizona. They're all different kinds of companies. Toys, T-shirts, laundromats, but it looks like most of them are tequila. Strange, but he must be one rich dude. Where'd you meet him? I'd snag that one if I were you."

"I don't even know him," Nina replied absently. El Paso, Texas. She'd been such a fool . . . such a naïve sap. She struggled to take a breath as her ribs closed around her lungs. She'd thought Ry was so kind and good, but she'd been wrong. Why had he wanted her in his home? To trap her? Had he been involved in her father's murder? Surely he was too young.

But what did she know?

Nothing.

Nothing about Shadow Creek.

Nothing about her father's death.

Nothing about Ry.

As much as it ripped her open to admit it, the facts remained—Ry had gone to Texas. Tony had businesses in Texas. Ry knew Tony, and Tony was named in the letter from H. Anderson. It could not all merely be coincidence.

Ry banged on the bedroom door. Nina had been locked in there for ages, and something was wrong. He could feel the ache in his bones.

"Nina! Hey, you all right in there?" Something in his absence had spooked her, he was sure. He willed himself to keep a clear head.

"Fine." Her voice was icy and distant—almost hesitant to speak to him. What had Harper done to her while he was gone? What had he told her?

Ry traipsed down the hall and sank onto the sofa cushion. As he put his feet on the coffee table, he noticed the book *War and Peace*. His heart stopped beating for a full five seconds. He tipped the book and shook it, open end down. No Nogales directions fell out.

Apprehension fisted around his gut. Had Nina found the note? Did she know about the shipment?

No!

He dropped the book on the floor, raced down the hall, and burst into the bedroom. Nina was perched on the end of the bed staring at him with huge startled eyes.

"Nina!" He knelt down and shook her shoulders gently. "I

mean, Nina," he said in a more relaxed tone, trying to slow his breathing. "Have you been reading *War and Peace?*"

"Well, yes. I . . ."

She catapulted from the bed and was out the front door before Ry had time to think what was happening. He bolted from the room and through the apartment, but when he threw open the front door, Nina was already gone.

Nina screeched her tires down the driveway, her pulse pounding against her temple as the startling truth crystallized in her mind. Ry had asked about *War and Peace.* Nogales. Tony. Nogales.

Tears stung the backs of her eyes, but she hardened her emotions and refused to let them fall.

Ry was a crook!

Swerving to the curb, she put the car in neutral and cut the engine. A car horn blared as a white pickup sped by, the driver yelling and shaking an angry finger at her.

Nina shrugged it off and fished through her purse looking for the note. She retrieved it. Tony Nogales it said. But it didn't mean Tony Nogales, did it?

"No." She answered her thoughts aloud. It meant Tony *in* Nogales. Tony Carlucci, no doubt. Ry was doing something with Tony Carlucci in Nogales. Arizona.

Speeding down the main road, heading to no place in particular, Nina's mind reeled. She supposed the best thing to do would be to turn it all over to the sheriff and let him deal with it.

But she couldn't do that, not with Wilbur Chase in the hospital.

Rich Willis sat in his parked rent-a-car and stared at the apartment. He checked his watch. He was hungry again. The airport hamburger hadn't really satisfied his appetite. Should he go to Ma & Pa's diner, or should he wait until Nina showed up?

Making a decision, he put the car in gear and eased onto the open road.

"So, you're back," Harper sneered.

"Glad to see you too," Ry replied through a sardonic twist of his mouth. Stopping to pour himself a cup of coffee, he turned to Harper. "Did you know why Tony wanted to see me?"

Harper broke out in a noticeable sweat, the beads of perspiration glistening on his forehead under the florescent light. "No. Why?"

"Why do I ask or why did he want to see me?"

"Don't try to confuse me with double-talk, Andies. Just tell me what's going on."

"He wants me to kill someone we all know very well." Ry arched an eyebrow in Harper's direction. It had the desired effect on the sheriff.

Harper plopped into the nearest chair. "Wh—what do you mean? Who?"

"He's really upset about the way things have been going— says that this town's full of incompetents and that something's got to give soon, or else."

Harper jumped to his feet. "But I thought it was the girl. I'm doing my best to keep tabs on everything. Heck, I had to poison Wilbur Chase. Thought the ol' geezer was going to die on me, or something. Did you tell Tony I've been trying? Did you?" His voice cracked on the last syllable, making his desperation more acute.

"You poisoned Wilbur Chase? That old guy in the wheelchair?" Ry put his cup on the counter, without having taken a sip, and got directly in Harper's face. "What did you do that for?"

"Tony told me to. Well, Tony told me to kill him, but I couldn't do that, so I just kind of put him out of commission for a while. I figured that was good enough since he can't do no talking anyhow." Harper leaned back in the chair more, widening the gap between himself and the face looming over him.

"Why's Tony worried about him? He can't hurt us."

"Ol' geezer's been talking to the Thomas chick. Tony thought we'd best be sure. You know?"

Ry bit out an expletive.

All the color drained from Harper's face. "You gonna kill me now?"

Ry gave Harper a light tap on the cheek. "No, Harper, I'm not going to kill you. I'm going to kill the girl."

As Nina sat on the sofa, a cloud of dust puffed around her. She choked and laughed at the same time. Here she sat in a dilapidated old cabin, afraid of her own shadow, for no reason, still without any real information about her father's death. She was no closer to finding out the reason or cause than she had been when she'd first read the letter from H. Anderson. All she'd discovered was more questions and heartache. She started to get up off the old sofa and then stopped mid-way.

What was that noise outside?

Ma & Pa's diner looked exactly the same as Rich remembered; not only the same as fifteen years ago, but also the same as when he was a boy. Sitting in this diner, where he had eaten many times before, would be his ultimate test. If he could enjoy a meal here without Ma recognizing him, then he owned safety.

He ordered a he-man sized chicken-fried steak and mashed potatoes and watched the comings and goings around him. As yet, no one had given him a second glance, and he was grateful of the fact. He remembered coming here with his grandfather. It had been a treat to sit at the counter and order a malted. The waitresses would dote on him as though he were an important adult. He smiled at the memory and wished life was still as simple and trouble free as it had been back then.

As Ma refilled his decaf, the door chimes rang out. Rich looked up to see Ry coming in. Ma immediately ran over to him, and Rich smiled. Still the same old Ma.

Ry sat at a booth at the opposite end of the restaurant and nodded and smiled politely at Rich as if to any stranger. Rich did the same, but inside he was anything but calm. Alarms were sounding in his head. His he-man sized steak arrived, and he inhaled it and got out of the diner as fast as possible. His nerves prickled, and he prayed he'd be able to pull this off.

Nina froze in place, her bottom hovering over the old sofa. There it was again! Someone outside. She could *feel* them.

Dragging in a silent breath, she crept to the closet and slipped behind the door.

Her heartbeat resounded in her ears like the percussion section of a marching band. It felt as if her heart would beat right out of her chest at any minute. Her breathing became unsteady as she found herself holding her breath for countless seconds at a time, trying to keep as quiet as possible—all the while, her strident heartbeat seemingly betraying her.

Then she heard the footfalls. Nearing the closet. She glanced down at her boots and wondered if they had heard her. Mutely she said a prayer as the closet door squeaked its discord at being opened. As the door opened wider, Nina flattened herself against the cedar wall. She held her breath, fearing the worst. Time stretched like a pulled elastic band, then snapped as a gloved hand snaked around the door and gripped Nina's arm like a vise. Her mouth fell open as she was yanked from the closet, and a tiny scream escaped her lips before darkness fell around her.

Chapter Thirteen

Nina awoke to absolute darkness, her eyes blindfolded and her hands cuffed in front. Bringing her hands to her eyes, she worked the blindfold, but it wouldn't come off. In fact, it seemed to squeeze her head even tighter. In a panic, she tried to stand and run, only to realize that her legs were bound at the shins.

For an eternity, she sat on the cold floor unable to think. Fear refused to give way to reason. Where was she? Who had abducted her and why? Well, come to think of it, she had a good idea of the *why*. She even had an idea of the *who*—although she still didn't want to believe it.

Moments later her prison began to move. The jarring did little to ease the throbbing knot on the front of her skull. Her head pounded, and the jostling only increased the pressure. Willing herself to ignore the pain, she decided to explore her prison.

On her hands and knees, she inched her way through the darkness, hoping to find an escape. Like an inchworm she accordioned herself along and found a smooth, cold, flat right angle going up from the floor. It was steel. She struggled to see through the blindfold to no avail.

Concentrating as much as her head would allow, she quit fighting for sight—something she found to be almost impossible. It seemed that regardless of how often she consciously told her mind that her eyes were blindfolded and useless, her brain still continued to struggle for control of her sight, but finally, her eyes were forgotten. Her nose and ears took control of the investigation.

She was in a vehicle—a very large vehicle, judging by how long it took her to inch her way to the right, to ultimately find another smooth, cold, flat right angle extending upward from the floor.

Suddenly, the vehicle lurched, and Nina was hurled to one side. A sharp pain shot through her hip as she kissed the unforgiving steel floor. She moaned. Trying to get back on her knees, she felt dirt particles along the bottom of the vehicle.

Listening to the grinding as the vehicle slowed abruptly then began to regain speed, she tried to count the gears shifting. With her head still pounding and her mind unaccustomed to processing information without sight, concentration became more difficult. But she finally deduced that she was in some type of eighteen-wheeler.

Knowing this did not ease her mind, except for the tiny speck of hope that a weigh station might open the truck for inspection and find her inside.

She drew in a deep breath. The hint of something . . . sweet? . . . wafted into her nostrils. She was unsure what it was. It just lingered there, the way strong perfume stays long after the person wearing it has left the room.

Rolling onto her hands and knees, she sniffed the floor for the scent. It smelled like . . . alcohol? It tickled her nose, but she took one more sniff, just to be sure. As she did, dust and something sharp pierced her nostril. She screamed and swatted her nose with her bound hands and then began to sneeze.

Whatever had stung her nose bounced off one knee and she clumsily fished for it.

Grabbing it between her palms, she felt along its slick edge. It was long and narrow and flimsy. It bent easily—so easily that it broke. She brought it to her nose and smelled it repeatedly until she finally recognized the scent. It smelled like grass or maybe . . . hay? Deciding to risk tasting it, she placed it between her teeth. Yes, it was definitely straw. Was she on a cattle truck?

Then, all movement stopped and Nina waited, motionless, for something awful to happen. A cacophony of clanging echoed through her prison and then light flooded in. She still could not see through the blindfold, but the blackness seemed less impenetrable.

She could hear heels pealing along the metal trailer as fear and anticipation froze her every movement—even her heart seemed to stop beating.

Roughly, she was yanked to her feet by one arm.

"Ouch," she cried. "You have to be so rough?"

"Just shut up and listen. I'm going to untie you. I'm going to take the blindfold off. I'm even going to uncuff you. But feel this?" He wrenched her cruelly and thrust her hands upon a holstered gun. "If you scream or try to get away, I'll shoot you. Any questions?"

Nina bobbed her head left and right, indicating she didn't.

He untied her legs, and for a split second, she thought about kicking him in the groin and trying to escape, but she was still handcuffed and blindfolded. She wouldn't get far before he would be able to stop her.

She shivered at the thought. She didn't want to die. No matter who had her, regardless of what terrible fate might be in store, she did not want to die, especially a death as violent as that.

He undid the blindfold next, and her eyes met the light reluctantly. She blinked rapidly, taking in her surroundings. She was in the trailer of a semi-truck, but not a cattle truck, so why had she found straw? She chanced a glance at her kidnapper. He donned a Shadow Creek Sheriff's Department uniform, but he did not look familiar to Nina. His dark hair was the color of coal, and his eyes were lifeless black holes. His olive skin showed the hint of a tan—one Nina suspected was of an all-year-round variety. He held his full mouth in a stern line, which made him look angry. His forehead was patterned with faint creases that gave him a rugged look that Nina decided was unappealing.

When he noticed her scrutiny, the creases in his brow deepened. Her knees began to shake and her fingers trembled. She wove them together and straightened her back. It wouldn't do to look the coward now, she decided.

"Why have I been taken?" she asked brazenly as he unlocked the handcuffs. "Are you really a deputy?"

"Don't ask questions. We're going to get out of the truck. We're going to walk arm in arm down the street. You're going to act like you've been in love with me for ages. Got it?"

"Do I have a choice?"

"You could choose to be shot."

"Great choice."

"All right then," he said with a crooked grin. "And remember, any false moves, and you're dead."

"I understand. You don't have to harp."

The man grabbed her hair and her head snapped back. Nina gasped, then bit her tongue to keep from crying out.

"Don't get smart with me. I don't think my boss would mind too much if you *did* end up dead. So don't tempt me."

Nina tried to nod, but he gripped her head in place. "Sorry," Nina choked out.

He led her to the back of the trailer where he jumped out first, then grabbed her arm and forced it down hard beside him. She stumbled and twisted her ankle, but his grasp kept her from falling completely.

"Stay on your feet," he bit out.

They walked down a busy street, which Nina discovered was Twenty-fourth Street. The sign, however, did not tell her what city they were in. Judging from the rows of traffic and the amount of eighteen-wheelers cruising the avenue, it was a major city, though.

The farther they walked, the more apprehensive she became, but also the more determined. She had traveled all the way to Shadow Creek to find a murderer; did she think it wouldn't be dangerous? Of course it would be. Now, abducted and coerced, even through her fear, she should take comfort in the fact that she was on the right track. She would discover the truth of what had happened to her father.

And she wouldn't be timid about it either. She couldn't afford to be.

Not any longer.

"Where are we?" she asked.

He tightened his grip on her hand he'd looped through his.

"Don't ask questions, I told you," he warned.

"Well, at least tell me your name. If we're supposed to be lovers don't you think I should at least know your name?"

"You don't know when to shut your mouth, do you?" He glowered down at her, but she refused to be afraid of him.

"Come on, surely you can see the logic in me having to know your name." She smiled at him sweetly, trying to smooth a little of his roughness.

"I guess since I'm probably going to kill you, it won't hurt for you to know my name."

Her nerve slipped, and she swallowed hard. Maybe she wasn't so tough after all.

He laughed at her. "Don't play with fire," he warned. "You might get burned."

Nina regained her nerve and smiled back at him. "So, what's your name?"

He sighed. "Jonah," he replied simply, then turned back toward the sidewalk.

"Well, Jonah, I can't say as I've ever seen so much traffic. How about you? Shadow Creek's an awfully small place."

He didn't answer.

"I happen to prefer small towns myself. Better for raising kids, don't you agree?"

Still no response.

"You married, or anything, Jonah? I wouldn't want to get caught holding hands and have some angry wife looking to knock me off. You know what I mean?" Nina looked up at him and smiled.

He didn't see her smile. He wasn't looking at her.

"Okay, Jonah. I'll be quiet."

"Thanks," he murmured.

She smiled at that and looked up at him again. "Did anyone ever tell you that you have a strong chin?"

He sighed heavily and glared at her. "It won't work."

"What won't work, Jonah? I don't know what you mean."

"You can't flatter me into letting you go. You can't croon my name and tell me how strong my chin is and expect it to affect me. I will not let you seduce me into not doing my job." He turned away from her again.

"Why, Jonah, I'm not trying to *seduce* you into anything. I'm not that sort of girl. I was merely trying to make friendly conversation. I mean, I have no idea how long we're going to be in each other's company, do I? I thought I'd just try to make friends. That's all." She eyed him coyly, but her efforts were wasted since, once again, he wasn't paying attention. She'd never been good at flirting, and now here she was, forcing herself to be sickly sweet, and he wasn't even looking at her! She had to get his attention, soften him, distract him from whatever he was supposed to do with her. It was her only chance of escape.

She studied him further. "What did you do to your shirt?" She fingered a torn section of his upper sleeve.

"Never mind!" He brushed her hand away. Maybe he was right. Maybe this wasn't going to work.

They crossed the street, and she saw the airport sign. Phoenix Sky Harbor. Reality and panic slammed her in the face. She stopped walking. Nobody would know where to find her. Her parents were on vacation and wouldn't even miss her until they returned. They—whoever *they* were—could cut her into tiny pieces and bury her in the desert somewhere, and nobody would even notice her disappearance. Oh, God, why hadn't she tried to contact her mother? Why hadn't she told her mother the whole truth? How long would it be before someone found out she was missing?

Jonah yanked her arm. "Come on. We don't have time for this! Move your feet," he hissed. "Or else!" Nina put one foot in front of the other.

As they entered the busy terminal, Nina contemplated whether she should scream and struggle, get some attention. He couldn't very well shoot her in front of all these witnesses.

As they approached the metal detectors, Jonah looked down at her. "Don't even think about it. I've got travel papers in my pocket for a prisoner I'm transporting by the name of Nina Thomas. If you run and I shoot you, it will be just another fatal escape attempt. Happens all the time."

"But . . ." Nina shook her head. "Never mind."

At security, Jonah explained that he was escorting Nina. He showed his badge and some other credentials that Nina could not make out. After making it through security, they made their way through a gate and proceeded toward a commuter plane. As they reached the jetway, Jonah stopped. With his hands on her shoulders, he turned her to face him.

"You're getting on that plane alone. No funny business. I'll be watching until you get into the air. Got it?"

Nina, the fear welling in her again, stifled a sob. "You're not coming? What about the airport? Won't they think that's odd?"

"Aw, that's so sweet that you're going to miss me."

He was ridiculing her, but he wasn't far off. It was absurd, she knew. After all, it was Jonah who had abducted and threatened to kill her, but for some reason, going alone was more frightening even than going with him.

"The pilot is armed with a dart gun. If you act up, he'll put you out for the duration, so be a good girl, huh?"

"You know, Jonah, you're not as bad a guy as you make out. I'd be willing to bet my life on that."

"Well, don't. The odds are against you. If you don't do what you're told, I won't hesitate to shoot you. Remember that if you get any wild ideas."

She smiled.

He didn't.

She turned and boarded the Beachcraft Bonanza, summoning all her strength not to look back at Jonah. She knew he would be watching until they got off the ground—he'd told her so. A shiver tremored through her body. Jonah would kill her if he had to.

Chapter Fourteen

Ry went into the apartment. Nina wasn't there. He cursed silently. He'd been hoping to talk to her—to set her straight on a few things. Even though she'd tried to disguise it, he knew she suspected him of some dreadful deeds. Ironic. She was leery of him, but evidently trusted Harper. He smiled wryly at the thought and then prayed she'd come back soon. He'd decided on the way home that he had to trust her with the truth. He was going to have to tell her who she could trust—tell her Rich would take her away. It was the only alternative, considering the twisted turn of events. Once she was safe in Virginia, he could finish the assignment without any more distractions or mishaps—hopefully.

He sat down to call Lottawalski, let him know what he planned to do, but the phone rang instead. Ry lifted the receiver. "Hello."

"Get to El Paso. Now."

"Mr. Carlucci? What's the matter?"

"Nothing. I've got a gift for you is all." He let out a short laugh. "Thought I'd make killing the girl a little easier on you."

The world stopped spinning. "Wh—what are you talking about?"

"Just get here and do the job, or you're both dead." *Click.*

Rich watched as Ry left the apartment. Nina still hadn't returned. It was beginning to make him nervous. A sinking feeling in his gut threw a warning up his esophagus, and he swallowed hard. He had to find Nina in a hurry. Time was running out. His gut told him so.

Ry drove off in a patrol car, and Rich followed at a discreet distance. Maybe *he* knew where Nina was. Maybe *he* was going to see her, and considering that Ry had told Lottawalski that Carlucci was getting suspicious, Ry would probably be grateful for the backup. Not that Rich could really help him, of course. He wasn't even officially part of the bureau. It was merely his friendship with Lance that had gotten him involved with this in the first place—well, that wasn't completely true. If he hadn't witnessed the execution of that DEA agent, then he'd still be living happily ever after. He laughed aloud. "Yeah, right! Happily ever after."

He pulled to the curb and watched as Ry stopped and made a phone call.

As he sat in the rental car, wondering why Ry would have to use a pay phone when there was a perfectly good phone at the apartment, Rich saw Sheriff Billy Ray Harper for the first time in over a decade. The sheriff walked right in front of the Ford, tipping his hat cordially. Rich smiled back and hoped the cosmetic surgery had worked.

Suddenly the sheriff stopped dead in his tracks and stared at Rich. Perspiration rose in beads on Rich's forehead as he held his breath and waited for the sheriff to move on. *Please move on,* Rich pleaded silently. *Please.*

His prayer went unanswered. Harper slowly moved to the driver's side of the Ford Taurus. Rich rolled the window down, and the sheriff leaned in. "Howdy."

"Hello, Officer," Rich said politely.

"Actually, it's 'Sheriff.' "

"Sorry."

"Nope. It's quite all right. Ain't too many civilians know the difference."

"Is there something I can do for you, Sheriff?"

"Not really. I just noticed you're driving a rental car. Where you up from?"

"Phoenix." Rich's voice sounded lifeless and hollow. He hoped Harper didn't notice. It seemed rather childish, being so agitated. When Rich had first met Billy Ray Harper, the sheriff had seemed very dedicated, homey, sincere, and many other generously gentle descriptions. But since that meeting over a decade ago, Rich had experienced another side to Billy Ray. A squeamish, sneaky, insecure side that made him mean and dangerous. All brawn and no guts, was how Rich described it. To him, any man with guts had the sense to be scared witless sometimes.

"You sightseeing or something?"

"Just traveling around. Seeing the Grand Canyon, Painted Desert, Meteor Crater, you know, stuff like that."

"What brings you to Shadow Creek?"

"Just passing through. Did I do something wrong, Sheriff?"

"Nope. Just keeping tabs is all. This is a quiet little town, and I'd like to keep it that way. Just check on strangers any time I get the chance." He stood erect and tipped his hat. "Enjoy your stay."

"I will, Sheriff." Rich watched Harper mosey on down the road. "I will," he repeated in a whisper.

With that on his mind, he watched Ry hang up and then get into the patrol car. Rich sped away from the curb and barreled past Ry at breakneck speed.

Ry watched the rental car race past him and recognized the signal. He flipped on the lights and siren and sped to catch up with the speeding car.

He eased up behind Rich as the Taurus rolled to a stop along the curb, then he approached the vehicle. "What's up?" he asked in a loud whisper when Rich rolled down the window.

"Where's Nina?"

"Don't know. I haven't seen her, but I'm really anxious to find her. She thinks I'm one of the bad guys."

"You've got to be kidding. That doesn't mean she trusts one of *them,* does it?"

Ry nodded. "Harper."

Rich groaned.

"Look, I don't know exactly what's going on, but she treated me like I had leprosy and then bolted from the apartment. Not only that, she had dinner with Harper and thinks he's all that." Ry hesitated to tell Rich the rest. The man wasn't going to take the news well. In fact, he might just kill Ry on the spot for letting things get this out of hand.

"What is it?"

Ry looked down the road and saw the sheriff's car heading their way. "There's no time now. I'm going to give you a ticket. Meet me at the cabin in twenty minutes. That's all the time I've got."

Ry scribbled a ticket, told Rich he could pay it at the courthouse, and then quickly disappeared into the patrol car before Harper had the chance to catch up with them.

Billy Ray Harper watched Andies tear the ticket from his pad and hand it to the stranger. There was something awfully familiar about that stranger and something awfully odd about him and Ry ending up together. *Maybe it's just my imagination,* he thought. But then again, maybe it wasn't. Maybe he should tell Tony about. If it turned out to be important, he could use the feather in his cap. A grin of satisfaction split his face at the thought of getting one over on Ry—finally!

Nina took one look at the pilot and knew she shouldn't cross him. His brooding stare and the scar across his cheek made him look like he'd been handpicked for a cops-and-robbers show, and when he didn't return her nervous smile, she decided not to speak to him at all. He wouldn't be a good conversationalist.

She wondered if he even knew how to fly the plane. She sat behind him, wringing her hands as the plane lifted off. Where were they going? Who were they going to? What would happen to her once they got there?

Nina's gut began to churn. She'd never been airsick, and she wished she'd have been able to stomach this trip. She desperately wanted to tell the pilot about her queasiness, but declined when she almost lost her lunch trying to stand up. Instead, she closed her eyes and said a silent prayer that lunch and dinner and anything else that happened to still be in her stomach would stay right where it was. After an agonizing and indiscriminate period of time, the plane finally touched solid ground. Nina's stomach still felt like it was in the clouds when a new bulldog shuffled her into a lengthy black limousine. He said something to the chauffeur as he locked her into the back, but she couldn't make out what it was.

A pitcher of water sat on the wet bar, but she'd have soaked herself trying to get a drink. Besides, she didn't think she could handle swallowing anything—even something as bland as water.

The dividing window lay open and, she could see in the

rearview mirror that the chauffeur had brown eyes and a mustache. Apart from that, and the fact that his hair was brown, she couldn't tell what he looked like. He didn't speak or turn around.

"Where are we going?" Nina asked tentatively.

He didn't respond so she asked a little louder, in case he hadn't heard. "Where are we going?"

"You've been told not to ask questions." His bass voice echoed through the vehicle, wracking Nina's body. For a second she was stunned.

"Well, it's not like I'm going to jump out of a moving vehicle once you tell me where I'm going. Plus, I'll know once I get there, so what's the big secret now?"

"Look, lady, I ain't telling you nothing, so just shut your trap."

"All right. I'll quit asking about our destination if you'll just talk to me about anything else. It's boring back here by myself."

"Shut up, lady."

The tears stung her eyelids, and she willed them to dry up. She may be scared, she may be uncertain, but there was no way she was going to allow these . . . these *scumbags* to get to her. She would be strong until the entire ordeal ended. Then she would shed uncountable tears—until there were no more tears to shed.

If only she were sure she'd live to release those tears, this all wouldn't be so frightening.

"I can't believe you gave me a ticket. Do you know I had to put up with that clerk flirting with me the whole time she filled out the paperwork. I thought that nosy busybody was going to figure out who I am."

"You know I had to give you that ticket. We had eyes." Ry leaned against a tree with his leg bent and his foot resting on the bark. He had changed into jeans and a blue shirt before heading for the rendezvous, ready to leave for El Paso as soon as he'd told Rich what was going on.

"Man!" Rich stood looking at the cabin that had once been a home. "I can't believe how much weather and time ruin things."

"Yeah, I know." Ry slapped Rich on the back. "Well, buddy, shall we go in and get the show on the road?" Ry walked ahead, then stopped and turned to face Rich.

"Look at this place. I just can't believe it." Rich stood in the doorway looking at the broken-down home. It was as much a shambles as his life. He turned his gaze to Ry. "So, why are we here?"

"I need to fill you in on a few things before I leave town. I figured this was the safest place to meet. No one even talks about this place anymore." Ry stood in the middle of the room looking around. When he turned back to Rich, the man wore a strange expression. "What's wrong?"

"I thought Nina might be here," Rich said quietly.

"Sorry, man. I don't think she remembers this place," Ry told him.

"I know she was young and doesn't remember much. I just had a feeling. I can't explain it. It's like being asleep in a fox-hole and knowing the enemy is approaching. You wake up just in time to shoot him before he slits your throat."

"Yeah. Dad told me that story about you and him and Lance. The Three Musketeers of Hanoi, right?" Scorn echoed in Ry's every word, but he couldn't help himself. Vietnam had screwed up a lot of guys, and his father hadn't been unsusceptible. It wasn't fair.

"Don't knock it, kid. Be grateful you haven't had to do battle. It ain't fun. Having to rely on buddies like Harry and Lance isn't something I ever want to do again, but I was sure glad to have them then. They saved my life more than once."

"Yeah, well, Dad isn't saving diddly anymore. You can't tell me a hero would blow his own brains out."

"You shouldn't be so bitter about it. And you shouldn't be so cynical, either. Harry may have done some rotten things after he joined Drug Enforcement, but don't ever doubt he was a hero in 'Nam. I couldn't have asked for a more devoted friend."

"A devoted friend that almost got you killed. With friends like that . . ."

Rich turned and walked out.

"Hey, I'm sorry. I didn't mean to get on the soapbox. It's just been rough, you know?" He knew he hadn't handled his father's suicide very well. He hadn't spoken to him for years prior—since the man's betrayal—and when Ry had heard about the suicide, the bitterness he had sown for so long had turned into a regret which completely confused him. His father was not only a crook, but a coward as well. Whatever heroic deeds he had accomplished in Vietnam were completely usurped by his choices afterward, yet the man was still his father.

He followed Rich outside. "I didn't even get to go to the funeral."

"Look at this." Rich was on his haunches looking at the fallen pine needles.

"Tire tracks?"

"Yeah and look." He pointed at the ground.

Ry crouched. "It's lipstick." He picked up the tube of lipstick, opened it and twisted the color to the top. "It's fresh. Nina was here." He stood. "She did remember this place."

Rich got up and walked to another spot.

"Rich, I need to tell you something."

But Rich wasn't listening. He was back on his haunches examining more evidence. "This is a man's print. It's too big for Nina's." He shook his head slowly. "Man, I don't like this. I don't like this at all."

"Rich, listen."

Rich stood and looked at Ry. "They've got her, don't they?" His voice was barely audible over the soft rustle of the trees, and Ry felt a stab of empathy go through his chest.

"That's what I've been trying to tell you. I've been ordered to kill her. My plane leaves in an hour."

Chapter Fifteen

The high chain-link gate slowly opened then closed behind the limousine. Nina's chest constricted. She knew who she was being taken to see—Tony Carlucci. She didn't know how she knew. She just knew, and the thought terrified her. The limousine eased to a halt in front of a huge warehouse, and the door opened.

A stocky Asian man greeted her. He was dressed in a very neat, double-breasted suit and alligator shoes. He took Nina's hands and unlocked the handcuffs. "I trust your journey was comfortable?"

"I was bound and blindfolded, then tossed around the empty trailer of a semi. I was held practically at gunpoint and told that if I didn't board a plane that I didn't have a ticket for, I'd be shot. I was handcuffed again, shoved into a limousine and had my request for directions refused. What do you suppose was comfortable about that?" A mixture of fear and rage made her mouth overrule her sense.

The man did not seem upset by her outburst, however. He

closed the door and stepped back for her to precede him. "My name is Ramon. I will be in charge of your visit with us."

"Ramon?" Nina stopped and turned to look at his Asian features.

He shrugged. "My mother is an Argentine," he revealed as if it were an everyday occurrence for him to explain his heritage. "Please continue this way."

Nina stepped cautiously into the warehouse. The building was huge with rows upon rows of stacked boxes from ceiling to floor.

Ramon took Nina's arm and led her into a small room off to one side of the warehouse. It was devoid of furniture, save a cot and a square wooden table.

"Is this to be my prison, Ramon?" Nina marched in and plopped indignantly onto the cot.

"This is our guest room, Miss Thomas. You will be showered with room service and maid service. I would hardly refer to it as a prison."

"Do you speak Chinese, Ramon?"

"No, Miss Thomas. My father is Japanese, and, yes, I do speak a little Japanese. Why do you ask?"

"And Spanish? Do you also speak Spanish?"

Ramon nodded.

"It must come in handy for a . . ." she searched for the word ". . . an *international businessman* like Mr. Carlucci to have such a multilingual asset on staff."

"I do not see the relevance of your inquiry, Miss Thomas."

"No relevance at all, Ramon. I was just making idle chit-chat."

"In that case, I shall leave you. Please note that there are no windows in this room. The door will be secure the minute I leave. So please don't try anything foolish." Ramon began to leave, but Nina stopped him.

"Ramon. Since this is my first night in this four-star establishment, would you mind joining me for dinner?"

"I would warn you to watch your tongue around Mr. Carlucci. He might not be as appreciative of your sarcastic wit as I, Miss Thomas."

"So it is Mr. Carlucci's . . . *hospitality* I have to thank for all this?" She opened her arms to take in the room.

Ramon closed the door, and Nina listened to the tumbler bolt as he locked it from the outside. In her solitude, she was about to let her tears have their way when she looked up and saw a video camera in the corner of the ceiling. She ripped off her boot and hurled it at the camera. "That's what I think of you, Mr. Tony Carlucci. That's what I think of you!" The light on the camera kept blinking.

The door flew open. Nina's head snapped from where she had bent down to retrieve her boot. A tall, lean man stood in the doorway. His thick, dark hair was only salted with gray, but his mustache and eyebrows were completely white. His smooth olive complexion seemed richer in contrast to the utter whiteness of the facial hair, making him classically handsome. His looks didn't phase Nina, but his presence made a knot form in her abdomen.

She straightened and slowly walked over to the cot, not once taking her gaze off the man. "You must be Mr. Carlucci," she said as she sat down.

"And you must be a fool!" He entered the room and slammed the door.

Nina started; her pulse began to race.

"I've killed people for less than ruining my equipment. Why did you do that?" The middle vein in his forehead throbbed, and as he spoke more rapidly, his Italian accent became more pronounced.

"I don't like being spied on," Nina replied evenly. She could feel the blood coursing through her jugular. She hoped he couldn't see it pulsating.

"Oh, you don't, do you? Well, too bad. You have lost the

freedom to choose. If you don't behave, you'll lose the freedom to breathe." He turned to walk out.

"Your sister is a very nice lady. Does she know her brother is a criminal?"

He stopped. When he turned to face her, his eyes were cold with ire. "What do you know about my sister?"

"Just that she's a very good cook, likes good literature, and loves her brother, Tony. I'd be willing to bet she doesn't know about you."

"And just what do you know, Miss Thomas?" His voice was calmer now.

Nina shook her head. "I know you just admitted to being a murderer."

He waved a hand, dismissing her assertion. "A mere misinterpretation of my statement, Miss Thomas. Don't you ever exaggerate to get your point across more effectively?"

"I don't think I've ever admitted to killing someone, no, Mr. Carlucci. But if it makes you feel better, I won't tell anyone what you said." She smiled at him.

"No. I know you won't." He shut the door behind him.

Nina listened to the lock turn before releasing the breath she'd been holding behind her "Miss America" grin. What was she doing? She could get herself killed being so cocky. But, then, he admitted to killing someone—plenty of someones probably—so the likelihood of him letting her live was pretty slim.

She shuddered at the thought, looked to the electronic eye, then to the door which held no hope of escape, and sighed. Flinging herself onto the cot, she lay with her arm across her face, wondering how she was going to get out of this predicament.

Sometime later, the tumblers in the lock churned.

She sat up and swiped away the moisture behind her eyelids. She refused to appear weak. She stood, just as the door swung open, and then collapsed back onto the cot when Ry stepped through the door carrying a cafeteria tray. "I've brought you something to eat, Miss Thomas."

Had he just called her "Miss Thomas?" A jumble of emotions washed over her as she sat staring at Ry, but she steeled herself. "I'm not hungry."

"Well, I'll just leave it, and you can eat whenever you're ready." He turned to leave.

"Ry? I mean, *Deputy Andies.*"

He looked back, and it seemed for a fleeting moment as if her words had struck a chord. He worked a muscle in his jaw and wouldn't properly meet her gaze. Nina didn't know what to think. "I need to use the restroom."

"I'll see what I can do." He disappeared behind the closed door. He was so cold. Distant. What had happened to the Ry who had rescued her? Her vision glazed as she stared at a spot on the floor, and her mind when numb.

When he came back, he carried a gun. "Sorry," he said, "but this is the way it's got to be." He even had the decency to look sorry. But Nina didn't believe he was. How could he be? He had rescued her, kissed her with tenderness—and urgency—and now was pointing a gun in her back. He couldn't be sorry.

He directed her to the opposite end of the warehouse, through a maze of ceiling-high stacks of crates. Stamped with stenciled letters in black ink, the crates read: CARANT TEQUILA. As they walked the aisles, Nina tried to rid her mind of Ry's betrayal and absorb as much as she could. There was an exit to the front—the door she had been brought in through. There were six loading bays to the back, two of which had semi trailers backed up to them, and an office up a set of metal stairs.

When she reached the bathroom and found it to be only a small cubicle, not unlike the cell she was being retained in, her hopes sailed out the window. Window! The bathroom did have a window and no electronic eye. Much to Nina's chagrin, however, the window was high above her head and had bars on the outside.

With her hopes for a viable means of escape dashed, she allowed Ry to escort her back to the room. How would she escape? She thought about Ry—how much she trusted him and how thoroughly he'd betrayed her. His duplicity was more crippling than her fright. He'd deceived her and lied. He'd never had any intention of helping her solve the mystery of her father's death. He'd merely intended for her to end up exactly where she was. But why? She still didn't understand it.

Lance Lottawalski sat in the airport terminal waiting for Rich. They were on their way to Texas. It had taken longer than expected to get everything ready for the raid that wasn't supposed to have happened for another couple of weeks. Rich was supposed to have gotten there and gotten her out so things could go as planned, but Carlucci had kidnapped Nina, forcing everyone's hands.

He thought about Ry, already in El Paso. They'd had no contact from him in hours. It was to be expected, but Lance hoped that Ry'd been able to do something to stall Carlucci's desire for Nina's death. If he hadn't, they might both already be dead. Carlucci wasn't going to let Ry get away with not killing her.

Lance let out a heavy breath. Everything was going to work out. He had confidence that Ry would figure something out. Ry was the Carlucci expert. He knew exactly what buttons to push.

Anthony Carlucci stormed through the door. "What's this?"

"What's wha—?" Nina stood in the corner, where she'd backed up to when the door flew open and scared her.

"This!" He was waving a piece of paper Nina recognized as the letter from H. Anderson. Carlucci tossed it onto the cot.

"What gave you the right to go through my purse?" Furious, she started toward him.

Carlucci closed the gap between them. "Don't answer my questions with questions," he bellowed. "I'm tired of your games. Now answer me!" He pushed her shoulder, making her stumble backward into the wall.

"It's a letter I got in the mail."

"When?" He screamed so loud Nina was sure he could be heard out the door and across the street.

"I—I don't know. I don't even know who H. Anderson is," Nina stammered, her bravado shattering. She felt the tears sting her eyes.

"No!" Carlucci roared, pointing an animated finger at her. "No tears! Who have you told about this?"

"No one. I swear."

"And what about this?" He shoved the note she had found stuffed in *War and Peace*. "What do you know about this?"

"Nothing! Really. I swear. Nothing." Nina sank to the floor with her knees raised and buried her face in her hands. She began to sob. "Honest. I don't know anything." Her voice sounded muffled underneath her palms.

"How do you know Ry Andies? What has he told you? Are you a Federal agent? Is he?"

Nina looked up at Carlucci in disbelief. "Am I a *what*?"

"Don't play dumb. A minute ago you were calling me a murderer, and now you act like an innocent child. Don't toy with me. It will only make me angry."

"You're already angry."

He let out a growl then picked her up by the arms and tossed her onto the cot. "I've about had it with you! Tell me all you know or I'll kill you with my bare hands."

Nina held her hands up in front of her. "I'm not a Federal

agent. I didn't know Ry before I went to Shadow Creek. I don't really know anything. Honest. I just wanted to find—"

Suddenly an explosion of gunfire shattered Carlucci's inquisition. Nina flung herself onto the floor.

Ry rushed in. "We got trouble."

She watched as Carlucci drew a gun from inside his jacket and inched out the door along the wall.

Ry looked at her and sent her a silent message with his eyes that she didn't comprehend. Then he turned, pulled a pistol out from somewhere, and inched out after Carlucci.

And he left the door open.

Nina crawled to the door and looked around. To her left, partway down a row of crates, a wounded man lay moaning in pain, a terrible high-pitched, agonizing howl.

The gunfire quieted. Nina decided to make a run for one of the loading bays. As she scrambled to her feet and darted out, Anthony Carlucci grabbed her arm. She screamed as he shoved her into Ry. "Keep the girl," Carlucci barked at Ry. "Kill her quick."

Ry spun her and wedged her back against his chest. He pinned her against him with his left arm around her neck with his right hand pressing a gun to her head.

The sound of glass breaking caused Nina to whip her head in the direction of the noise.

"No fast moves, Nina, okay?" Ry's breath danced across her ear, and something inside Nina died a little. After all this, she still wanted him to be her knight, and here he was with a gun to her head.

Even though his tone didn't sound threatening, Nina didn't respond. She just stared at a fallen crate of tequila. Bottles lay smashed, while straw and splintered wood and glass lay in a sea of alcohol. Looking more closely, Nina gasped. She could see white powder mixing with the liquid.

"Be still!" Ry's voice held a raspy urgency that frightened Nina. Nina stopped breathing. Carlucci was watching them.

"Kill her now, Ry." Carlucci raised his arm and pointed his gun at them.

"Mr. Carlucci—"

"Now! Or I'll shoot you both."

Frozen with terror, Nina watched helplessly as a man in a blue suit rose from behind a forklift that was parked in the middle of the gangway. "All right, Carlucci, give it up," he said. Carlucci swung around, aimed at the man, and fired three times. The man ducked behind the forklift, unscathed.

"Give it up!" He yelled from his concealed spot. The man eased out from behind the machine. Carlucci fired again and missed.

Ry was whispering something in her ear, but she didn't realize it until it was too late. The gun barrel to her temple started to move.

Carlucci whirled to face them.

Bang!

Bang!

Two shots rang out. Carlucci slumped to the ground. And then, Nina felt herself falling. She was suddenly free, and Ry lay on the ground at her feet. Blood pooled around her foot.

Nausea rose up and, in the next instant, she felt a searing pain under her chin. Blood began to flow. She looked down at Ry and saw the bullet wound in his chest. It was amazing, she thought, such a small hole and the blood—it seemed to be coming from her body, not his.

Slowly, she dragged her hand to her chin, and then looked at her blood-soaked fingers. She went dizzy then everything went black.

* * *

Federal Agent Harold Rylan Anderson, Jr., lay in the intensive care unit of Thomason Hospital. The bullet had split his rib cage and punctured his right lung. Still he clung to life. Glucose and medication were being administered intravenously and a respirator assured his breathing, but he was alive.

Consciousness came to him in an unpredictable ebb and flow. He saw shadows of Rich and Lance Lottawalski and tried to smile. He was tough. He would fight. He would win. He wanted to let them know; they looked frightened, helpless. But he wasn't even sure if the smile actually reached his mouth or if it got lost somewhere on the journey from his brain.

Rich sat in the hallway on a hard, uncomfortable bench. Ry's blood stained Rich's clothing. He kept staring at it as if the reminder could help him cope with what might happen. Rich looked up to see Lottawalski coming down the hall with two cups of coffee.

He perched on the bench next to Rich. "You look like crap," he said, handing Rich a styrofoam cup.

Rich sipped some of the coffee and grimaced. "Wrong cup. This has sugar in it."

"Oh, sorry."

They switched cups. "Much better."

"You, or the coffee?" Lance asked.

"The coffee. I think it's going to be a long time before I'm better." Rich sighed. "At least Nina is going to be okay." He turned a steely gaze to his friend. "And at least Carlucci is dead."

"I'm going to ignore your attitude, Rich. I know that's your emotions talking . . ."

"C'mon, Lancelot. He didn't even suffer. You know he deserves worse than he got. He was going to kill Nina—and Ry. We should have assassinated him fifteen years ago. Think of how much pain and suffering we would have saved if we had."

"I know how you feel, buddy, but you sound so cold."

Rich put his cup on the floor between his feet. "I know it, but it's how I feel right now. Ry's lying there in a hospital bed fighting for his life. Carlucci deserved to suffer."

"You need to concentrate on Ry right now, not Carlucci. I still can't believe you took the shot."

"Well, Lance, I was nervous, I can tell you. But I saw his laser on her and decided I had to do something before he got off another round. I never dreamed I'd make him hit her. I almost had a frigging heart attack when I saw her bleeding." Rich shuddered at the memory.

"I know. You were ash-gray when I walked over. You should have seen your face." Lance chuckled.

"She's going to be okay; that's all that matters. Well, that and the fact I finally got Carlucci." He couldn't believe the relief he found in knowing Carlucci was no longer a threat. He only wished Harry had been alive to celebrate with them. "You know, it's kind of funny how you excuse your friends so many things you'd want to kill your enemies for."

"For instance?"

Lance followed as Rich got up and started down the corridor to Nina's room.

"Just thinking about Harry. I mean, when you think about it, I should hate him for almost killing me and Nina and making me live in hiding all these years, but I don't. We were buddies so tight before he went off the deep end that the only one I blame is Carlucci. If he hadn't lured Harry with all the lies, all the money, none of this would've ever happened."

Rich pushed open the heavy door and peered around it to Nina lying in bed. "Hey! She's moving."

Ry drifted into consciousness an innumerable number of times that day. A nurse hovered over him, checking some tubes or something—he couldn't really tell. He tried to speak to her, but his voice was a hoarse, indecipherable groan. She patted him on the hand and told him to rest. She smiled and left.

He didn't want to rest. He wanted to ask questions. Was he going to survive, or was this sea between sleep and wakefulness a cruel joke God had decided to play on him before the Grim Reaper finally came to pick him up?

The nurse came back in and put something in the IV unit. Ry watched her, wanting to ask what she was doing. He hoped it was something that would clear his head so he could speak. He needed to get a message to Lance and to Rich. He needed to find out what had happened to Nina. Ry's mind tried to concentrate. He wanted to see Nina again—explain his real role in all this. The thought of her being afraid of him was awful—much worse than the physical pain from the gunshot. He couldn't concentrate on much, but the image of Nina's frightened eyes haunted him. But he hadn't had a choice. He'd had to put that gun to her head. If he hadn't, Carlucci would have done it for him.

What had happened to Carlucci? Ry's brain refused to work.

Whatever the nurse had injected didn't have the desired effect. His head became more cloudy, regardless of how he tried to focus on his thoughts.

Sleep claimed him once more.

Chapter Sixteen

R_y awoke in a different room. He looked around and watched the monitor bounce up and down to the rhythm of his heartbeat. *At least I'm still alive,* he thought wryly. He smiled and almost chuckled, but the searing pain forced him to stop.

He scanned the room. He was definitely still in the hospital, but since he wasn't attached to as many tubes and this wasn't the morgue, he must be getting better. The clouding of his mind seemed to be lifting.

A doctor came in—correction, a beautiful doctor came in—and Ry smiled at her weakly. She glided to his bedside, but he wasn't sure if she actually glided or if his cloudy mind was playing tricks on him. He decided after a moment that it must be his mind, or the medication, or something, because her auburn hair bounced in slow-motion curls off her shoulders as she approached him.

"Good to see you, Ry. How are you feeling?"

"You tell me, Doc."

"Still a little light-headed?" She perched on the edge of the bed.

"I guess. It looked to me as if you glided into the room."

"And you don't think I'm that graceful?" She sent him a teasing smile.

"Well, it's not . . ."

She held up her hand to interrupt him. "Trust me, I'm not. It's the medication that's making you feel that way, coupled with the fact that you've been on a liquid diet for quite a while."

"Am I going to be okay?"

She nodded. "You'll have to be my guest for a while, but you'll recover nicely."

"Where am I?"

"Flagstaff Medical Center—"

"Flagstaff, but I thought—"

"You were transferred here from Thomason in El Paso after you stabilized."

"I have to talk to my boss. It's urgent."

She shook her head. "No."

"But you don't understand . . ."

"I'm supposed to tell you that everything is fine in Shadow Creek."

"It is?"

"Apparently," she told him. "Mr. Lottawalski said he couldn't give me the details, but to reassure you as soon as you were stable."

"Thanks, Doc."

"Here. Take this." She handed him a pill and a paper cup full of water. "It will help you rest."

He took the medication in his hand. "Don't you think I've rested enough?"

"Take the medication," she prompted, "and if you're a good boy, I'll bring you some solid food when you wake up."

She smiled, and Ry swallowed the pill.

* * *

Nina slowly awakened. Her mind felt as foggy as her eyesight. She moved her gaze around the room trying to recognize her surroundings. When her eyes finally cleared, she knew she was in Shadow Creek, in Ry's bedroom. She turned her head to one side and noted two men—two strangers. Startled, she quickly tried to sit up, only to find her head spun like a child's toy top.

"No, no. Lie still. You're going to be all right," the balding one said.

"Who are you? You were at the warehouse. How did we get here? What . . ." Nina's voice gave out as the dryness in her throat made her cough.

"Whoa! You need to take it easy. Don't ask so many questions. You need to concentrate on getting better."

"But . . ." Nina croaked.

"No 'buts.' My name is Lance Lottawalski. You got a nasty cut under your chin when Carlucci—that is, when Anthony Carlucci's gun fired."

Nina lifted a heavy hand to her chin. Eventually, her hand reached the thick bandage.

"Eighteen stitches," Lance informed her. "But you're going to be okay. You gave us a scare, though."

"How long have I been unconscious?"

"Oh, it's been almost a week since you were injured. You were in the hospital for a few days for observation. They kept you pretty well sedated. Then we flew you here so you'd be in a semi-familiar place when you woke up."

"My mother . . ."

"We haven't informed her yet. As soon as we knew there was no danger, we thought you'd personally like to tell her about your little misadventure."

"I'm hungry."

"Good. I'll get you some soup or something, but only if

you promise to quit asking questions for a while." He gave her a fatherly smile, and she nodded her acceptance of his terms.

He disappeared out the door. The other man—the one who had remained completely silent—followed him.

Rich was on his way to Flagstaff. He had a hotel reservation at the Ramada Inn. He would check on Ry, stay a few days, and then fly home to Virginia. He felt like a fool. He'd wanted to talk to Nina, to explain everything to her, but he'd been afraid to open his mouth. She had her own life to live. He didn't need to complicate matters. He couldn't even be sure if she would want to know the truth. Sure, she'd gone to Shadow Creek looking for answers. But she had been looking for answers for a *death*. What was he supposed to do? Walk up and shake hands, then tell her the entire story? He couldn't do it.

Nina devoured a bowl of potato soup. "Where'd you get this?" she asked Lance, who had brought a kitchen chair into the bedroom.

"I made it."

"It was good." She looked at him, her brow creased. "Is Ry in jail?"

"Jail?" The surprise in Lance's voice didn't go unnoticed, but it confused Nina.

"Yes, jail. You know, where they put the bad guys?"

"I know what jail is." He leaned forward. "Why would Ry be there?"

"Because he almost got me killed. Because whatever illegal things Anthony Carlucci was into, Ry was helping him with. In short, because he's a bad guy." Nina brought her hand to her mouth, and then winced at the pain it caused her chin.

"Be careful. You don't want to rip your stitches," Lance warned. "Ry isn't a bad guy."

"Then why was he hanging around Anthony Carlucci? He was in El Paso with Carlucci, wasn't he?"

"I wasn't going to tell you the entire story right away, but since you're so anxious . . ." He got up and walked behind the chair. Resting his hands on the back of it, he began to speak again. Nina listened. "Ry is an FBI agent . . ."

"You mean—"

Lance cut her off. "Yes." He nodded. "He's FBI; I'm FBI. We've been after Carlucci for a long time. You, young lady . . ." he pointed an index finger at her, ". . . almost blew the whole deal. That's why Ry was trying to keep tabs on you. He didn't want you to end up dead."

"But I thought that *he* was going to kill me." Nina shook her head in disbelief of her own mistake.

"Well, had Carlucci had his way, Ry would've killed you. Of course, we think Carlucci ordered the hit on purpose. We think he was already suspicious of Ry by then."

"But I still never found out about my father's death. You see, I got this letter signed H. Anderson that said he was responsible. That's why I came to Shadow Creek in the first place. Because I found out that the accident wasn't an accident. I just had to find out why and who. I still don't know how Carlucci was involved."

"I know. I know all about the letter. I retrieved it from the El Paso warehouse."

"Carlucci was into something highly illegal, wasn't he? What was it? Drugs? I thought I saw something in the warehouse that looked like cocaine. Was it? Or was he into something else? Murder, perhaps? Assassination of a president? What?"

"Criminy, you've got an imagination, don't you?" He picked up the empty soup bowl from the bedside table. "I've got dishes to do, and you need some rest. We'll talk later."

* * *

"Thanks," Ry said as Rich handed him a pot of chrysanthe-mums. "Couldn't find a *NASCAR Scene*, huh?" he teased.

"Sorry. You're lucky you got those. I didn't think about it un-til I was already here. I had to get what I could." Rich brought up a chair and sat beside the hospital bed. "You sure look a lot better than before."

"Yeah, well, the doc says I'm going to live."

"Bet if you could've seen that doctor while you were un-conscious you'd have come round a lot sooner."

Ry chuckled and tried to sound nonchalant. "Yeah. She's a looker." Really, though, he was thinking that there wasn't a woman in the world who compared to Nina, but he couldn't very well tell that to Rich. "How's Nina?" he asked instead.

"She's okay. She might have a scar, but it's right at the jaw line. Not too noticeable."

"You going to tell me what happened? Who shot me? D'you ever find out?"

Rich shook his head. "It was either Harper or Martinelli, I'm pretty sure, but we don't know for a fact. We'll find out some-how. 'Course, they're all going down for a long time anyway. You gathered enough information to send them packing for a lifetime, and with Carlucci dead, the whole cartel will fizzle out, I'm sure."

"Where's Lancelot?"

"Oh, he sends his regards. He's staying with Nina at your place in Shadow Creek."

"She still think I'm a crook?"

Rich shrugged. "Don't know. I left before she had a chance to tell us anything. Lancelot will get the scoop."

Ry raised an eyebrow. "You left before she had a chance to talk? How come? I would have thought you'd have told her the whole deal before you ever let her out of your sight."

Rich focused on the floor tiles. "I wimped out." He glanced

at Ry sheepishly. "What if she doesn't really want to know the truth?"

"C'mon, man. She risked her life to find out the truth. What makes you think she'd run from it now?"

"She didn't know she was risking her life," Rich reasoned.

"Time's up, gentlemen." The two men turned to see the nurse standing in the doorway. "Mr. Anderson, here, needs his rest. You can come back tomorrow."

"Saved by the bell," Rich said. He stood and crossed the room to the door. "See ya, buddy."

Nina awoke to a beautiful dawn. She hobbled out of bed and pulled back the curtain to absorb the beauty of the morning. The sky was a wisp of grays and blues in the misty morning haze, the sun not yet visible on the horizon. She'd been in bed for nearly a week, and it had seemed absurd considering her only injury was a cut on her chin.

What Nina hadn't realized until Lance had told her, was that the "cut" had been a bullet lodged in her jawbone that had to be surgically removed.

She moved away from the window and chose clothes for the day. Deciding to go for a walk, she chose her Reeboks, blue jeans, and a plain blouse. She slipped on her robe, and then headed out the door toward the bathroom.

"You're up and at 'em early." Lance's voice greeted her from the living room.

"I just thought I'd get cleaned up and go for a walk," she called back.

"I'll fix you some breakfast before you go."

"No need."

"Yes need. Go and get dressed. It'll be ready when you are."

The warm shower felt good to Nina. She thought about the

room Carlucci had kept her in. It hadn't been dirty, but being away from there certainly made her feel cleaner.

She shuddered at the thought of how close she had come to dying. Why Carlucci had been so upset by her presence remained a mystery to her. Somehow, he must have been involved in her father's accident, she supposed. Perhaps he'd ordered the murder. *But would he have needed an eight-year-old girl dead also?* Nina thought deeply. Maybe she knew something she wasn't supposed to know. Maybe if she ever remembered properly, she'd know what it was.

Once again, thoughts of Ry filtered into her mind. She'd completely misjudged him. The entire time she'd doubted him, he'd been trying to save her, not harm her. It would've been nice if he'd said something. A smile curved her lips. Maybe he had been sincere the night he'd taken her in his arms and comforted her.

Or maybe he'd just been doing his job. The water turned icy and Nina turned off the taps. After drying off and getting dressed, she combed her hair and went into the kitchen. Lance stood over the stove.

"Mmm. Smells good," Nina said, sitting at the table. "Can I help?"

"I like the way you sit down before you ask if you can help," Lance teased. "No, you can't help." He turned to face her. "You hungry?"

"Now that I smell it I am."

Much to Nina's disappointment, Lance left her alone to eat. She inhaled four strips of bacon and two eggs so quickly she surprised even herself.

"You must've been hungry," Lance said when Nina appeared in the living room. "That's a good sign."

Nina sat down in the chair next to the couch Lance was resting on. "Do FBI agents usually play nursemaid to gunshot victims?"

He smiled at her. "You're a special case."

"How so?"

"You're like family to me. I took the time to be able to make sure you're okay."

Family? How could she be like family? She didn't even know this man. There were still things she didn't know. "What else can you tell me?"

"About what?" He wanted to avoid the issue, she could tell. He barely looked at her when he spoke.

"What don't you want me to know?"

"Nothing. Ask me a question, and I'll give you an answer." He looked at her pointedly.

"Why did Carlucci want me dead?"

"Because you were digging too deep. He didn't want to be held accountable for your father's accident."

"So it was him. Why did he want my dad dead?"

Lance shook his head. "Your father didn't want you to know any of this. He wanted you to be safe from harm. I suppose it doesn't really matter now.

"Your father witnessed an execution. The execution of a Shadow Creek deputy sheriff and an undercover DEA agent."

"So Carlucci had him killed to shut him up?" She leveled her gaze on Lance. He seemed a little uncomfortable, rigid.

His Adam's apple bobbed up and down, and then he gave her a slight shrug. "I can't really tell you much more."

"Can't or won't?"

"Look, Nina, you're safe, your father is . . ."

"Is what?"

"*Avenged.* He lost his life because of this scumbag, and now everything is set to rights."

"But—"

He leaned toward her. "You wanted answers, you got answers. The bad guy got what was coming to him, and justice is served. You should go home and forget about all this. You have your whole life ahead of you. Don't spend it looking back."

"Sounds like something a dad would say."

"If he were sitting here right now, I'm sure your dad *would* say it. He and I were pretty tight. I know for a fact he wouldn't want you dwelling on the past."

"I guess you're right." Maybe it was better just to let go.

He let out a snort. "Guess? You guess?"

She laughed at the face he made. "Okay, you're right." She stood and zipped her windbreaker. "I'm going for a jog. Do you want to come along?"

He shook his head in reply. "I'm not dressed for it."

Nina nodded. "Do you always wear a blue . . . ?" Her legs went weak, and Lance rushed to her.

"Are you all right? You look as if you've seen a ghost."

She squinted to focus properly on his face. "Do you always wear . . ." she cleared her throat, ". . . a blue suit?"

He looked down at his clothing. "Yeah, I do. That way I don't have to spend time deciding what to put on. Why?" He looked puzzled.

"J—just wondering." She turned away from him. "I'm going to lie down."

"Wait a minute." He grabbed her arm. "Are you sure you're okay?"

"I'm sure." Nina went down the hallway into the bedroom.

Chapter Seventeen

Nina studied her scar in the mirror. She smiled crookedly. No use worrying about it, she decided. Besides, it would be a conversation piece when she got older—and, at least now, she would be getting older.

She combed her hair and smoothed out her dress before leaving the bathroom. It was a beautiful sun-yellow rayon shift that she'd purchased especially for today. As she thought about going to see Ry, her stomach began to flutter. Seeing him would be awkward. She felt silly for having doubted him. She should have believed him. She should have recognized his concern as sincere. She should have trusted her own instincts, if nothing else.

She hurried down the hall. "Lance, I'm ready," she called.

"I'm in the kitchen."

Nina entered the kitchen at a trot and then came to a dead stop at the doorway. Lance was not alone. Another man sat with him—the man who had been there when Nina had first regained consciousness. "Hi," she said uneasily.

"Hello." His voice resounded deeply, but gently. It reminded her of her father—or rather, what she thought her father sounded like.

"Nina?" She looked at Lance. "This is Rich Willis. He was with us in El Paso."

Nina looked back at Rich. "Oh. You helped, then?" She approached the table where the two men sat, and then held out her right hand. "Nice to meet you, Mr. Willis."

"I . . . I . . ."

"Rich shot Carlucci."

"I'm sorry about your jaw," Rich told her.

She touched the scar and shrugged her shoulders. "Better than being dead." She sat down. "He would have, you know?"

Rich nodded. "I know; that's why I did it."

"The other day, when you asked me about my suit?" Nina nodded and Lance continued. "Why was that significant?"

"It's nothing really," she told him.

"I think it is something. That's why Rich is here."

She turned to Rich. "Are you a shrink or something?"

"No, he's not a shrink," Lance said, sounding surprised at her conclusion. "Tell me about my suit."

Nina sighed. "It's silly, really. It's just that ever since I was a kid, I've had this vision of a man in a blue suit. He took my dad into a helicopter, and they flew to heaven."

"What?!" Nina glanced at Mr. Willis, who looked whiter than enriched flour.

"I know. Pretty dumb, huh?"

"You ready to tell her now?" Lance was asking Mr. Willis.

"Tell me what?"

Lance tapped Rich on the arm. "You ready?"

Rich nodded, but Lance spoke.

"Remember I told you that your father witnessed a double murder?" Nina nodded. "Well, what I didn't tell you was that after your father witnessed the killing, he called me. We were buddies in Vietnam—saved each other's lives more than once." Lance stood up and began to walk across the kitchen tile. "I knew something was up immediately. Pete wouldn't have called me if it wasn't important, so I got on it immediately."

He went to the sink and poured himself a glass of water. Without offering any to Nina or Rich, he continued his story. "We didn't have anything at the Bureau, so I called the DEA. When I explained about your dad, they told me they had an agent down but that another was still in place. They said he hadn't been there long—I can't remember, six months or so—but that he was in pretty tight. His name was Harold Rylan Anderson." He sipped his water.

"H. Anderson? *He* wrote me the letter. He said he was responsible for my father's death."

Lance nodded. "He was, in a way." He glanced at Rich. "Right?"

Rich nodded noncommittally.

And then Lance's words penetrated completely. "Wait," she said. "Harold *Rylan* Aderson? As in *Ry*?"

Lance gave her a slight nod. "Ry's father."

"But—"

Lance came and put a gentle hand on her shoulder. "That's something Ry has to come to terms with on his own. Don't blame the son for the sins of the father. Ry's nothing like what Harry became."

Nina forced herself to keep breathing normally. H. Anderson was Ry's father? She swallowed hard and gazed at Lance, silently telling him to go on with the story.

"Anyway," Lance continued, "Harry was working both ends of the stick. He got really caught up in Carlucci's game. It isn't hard to do, I suppose, when you see all that money and how easy it is to smuggle coke into the country." He looked at the tile and shook his head wistfully. "Shame, really."

"Go on," Nina urged, not wanting him to get off track.

Lance began to pace again. "Of course, his superiors trusted him. He'd been doing undercover work for years. Anyway, they told Harry to watch out for your dad in case Carlucci got wind of a witness. I guess Harry didn't want his icing licked, so he told Carlucci about Pete." Lance placed his glass in the sink and then turned to look at Nina. "We were already planning to relocate you and your father, just in case we needed him to testify. Harry got wind of it, and tipped off Carlucci." He sat down. "I guess we should've known something was up with Harry. He never gave us enough to bust anybody—kept saying he needed more time. He finally went insane . . ."

"So they got to us first?" Nina felt the impatience pricking her. Lance wasn't talking fast enough.

"Not exactly. I came to Shadow Creek to help you move. We were on our way out of town when a car ran us off the road. We were never sure—until Harry killed himself—that it was an attempted hit, but we didn't take any chances."

"You were there?" She glanced from Lance to Rich, then back to Lance.

Lance nodded. "You were hurt pretty bad, but we knew you'd make it."

"And you went with Dad's body? In a helicopter? That's why I remember a helicopter—and you?"

"I went with your dad, yes, but he wasn't dead, Nina."

Silence shrouded the room. Nina stood, the sound of the chair scraping across the floor shattering the silence with a squeaky wail. She shuffled backward, toward the doorway. "Not dead? What do you mean not dead?"

"I mean, he's not dead," Lance replied simply.

"You mean he's *not dead*? Where is he, then? Huh? Where is he?" She glared at Rich, who started to perspire. She felt sick to her stomach. Bile rose in her throat then dissipated.

Lance looked at Rich. Rich looked at Lance, then at Nina.

Nina studied them both, and then the truth dawned. She flung an index finger at Rich. "You? Oh my—!" She turned, ran to the bedroom, and slammed the door.

"I told you it was a mistake," Rich said decisively.

"It wasn't a mistake. It was a shock. Come on, Rich, she's believed you were dead for most of her life. You didn't expect open arms right away, did you?"

Rich shook his head. "She hates me. She thinks I deserted her. I know she does. I know I do."

Lance put a consoling hand on his friend's shoulder. "She doesn't hate you. She needs time to adjust. Why don't you wait a few minutes and then go in and talk to her?"

"She doesn't want me to talk to her. I don't know why I let you and Ry talk me into this. I should've stayed dead. It would've been better for everybody."

"No, it wouldn't. I know how much you've wanted to see her over the years. Can you honestly tell me that it would've been easier to let her go again?" Lance sat down and looked earnestly at his friend.

"I shouldn't have let her go in the first place. I should've kept her with me." Rich got up, walked to the sink, and stared out the window at nothing in particular. "She's my daughter. I shouldn't have given up on her."

"We've been over this umpteen times in the past. You did the right thing. It was best for Nina—safer. It was best for you. It was more believable that only you had died. It kept your cover, and you know it."

"But . . ."

"No excuses. Go in there and talk to her," Lance pressed.

Rich sighed. "I don't know."

Nina lay on the bed, tears streaming down her face. How could he have done this to her? She couldn't pick an emotion.

Happiness, sadness, anger all pierced her heart like a thousand swords. So many times during her childhood she had dreamed of her father still being alive. Now that it was a reality, she felt cheated and lost. He had left her—not without choice, as she had always believed—but of his own free will.

Rejected.

That's what she felt—rejected.

She sat up and slapped away tears that defiantly kept falling.

Jonah Martinelli sat in the interviewing room of FBI Headquarters. Special Agent Rex Woodrow, a large, burly black man, had been trying to get Jonah to talk. He wasn't spilling it. The Feds already had enough information and evidence to put him up for a long time. He knew it. They knew it. Everybody knew it. And Jonah wasn't a stool pigeon.

"Come on, Martinelli. You know it's all over. Why are you fighting us on this?"

"Can I have a piece of paper and a pen?" Martinelli leaned back in the wooden chair, raising the front legs off the floor.

"You want to write your confession?"

"Can I have it, *please*?"

Woodrow walked to the door, knocked on the tiny observation window and yelled. "Get us a pen and some paper." He turned back to Jonah. "This better be good, Martinelli."

A yellow notepad and a pencil passed through the door, and Woodrow sat opposite Jonah while he composed a letter.

"You think I could have some privacy? It's kind of hard to write with somebody watching you." His disgust for Woodrow was palpable.

"No, you can't have privacy. If you wanted privacy you should have stayed on the right side of the law. Besides, there's going to be a lot more than one man next to you where you're going. Consider this a lesson," Woodrow replied snidely.

"Are all agents jerks, or did you corner the market?"

Woodrow sprang to his feet. "Watch your mouth or I'll have you scrubbing out the prison john with your toothbrush."

Jonah ignored the threat and went about composing his letter.

Rich was about to knock on the door when it flew open, startling both him and Nina. She stared at him, her mouth open. "You should close your mouth before a fly goes in," he said, trying to lighten the tension.

She burst into tears and ran to the bed.

"I'm sorry. I'm so sorry," he said, following her into the room and sitting next to her.

"You used to say that to me all the time, didn't you?" She had her back to him, face buried in a pillow so her voice was muffled and difficult to understand.

He nodded then, realizing she couldn't hear a nod, said. "Yes. I wasn't thinking. I'm sorry."

She sat up and looked at him. "Why?" she asked simply.

"I didn't want you on the run the rest of your life. It looked more realistic that only one of us survived," he replied instinctively.

"But how did you know they wouldn't come after me anyway?"

"I didn't. I took the chance that Carlucci wouldn't feel the need to kill an innocent child. I knew he was capable of murder. I knew he'd even kill a child. But I also knew that he understood *I* was the witness, not you. I took the chance that he wouldn't harm you as long as he wasn't backed into a corner."

"But . . ."

Rich shook his head. "If he'd ever found us, he'd have kidnapped you to get to me. Don't you understand that?"

Nina nodded.

"I didn't want to leave you, Nina. Truly, I did it only for your safety."

Tears welled in his eyes and melted Nina's heart. She nodded again, in silent understanding. "Okay," she said softly. "Let's start over, huh?"

He looked at her, relief glistening in his eyes. "You don't hate me?"

"I've wished you were alive for fifteen years. I'd be a fool to cast you off now, wouldn't I?"

Sheriff Billy Ray Harper—*Ex*-Sheriff Harper—sat in his jail cell alone. Tears came to his eyes as he thought about Irene's face when she'd learned about the death of her brother and that her husband was going to jail. He'd feared she would have a heart attack. He really did love her, he supposed, but now he couldn't decide if he felt more sorry for her or for himself. He was going to prison. *She* only had to adjust to that fact; *he* actually had to live it.

Irene hated him now. She had spat on the ground at his feet. He was sure she blamed him for Tony's death. Why didn't she blame *Tony* for *his* prison sentence? Why was it never anybody else's fault?

He looked up and glanced at the agent walking up to the cell. "Time to go," the man told Harper.

"Where're we going?"

"Don't ask questions."

Harper was led into the interviewing room. The man who escorted him told him to sit down. The man didn't look as if he was in a very good mood.

"All right, Harper, I have in my hand . . ." he held up a piece of paper ". . . a confession from Jonah Martinelli. He's told us practically everything, and we're going to go easy on him," Woodrow said.

"So what do you want from me?" Harper tried to sound tough, but the perspiration collected in his armpits.

"Well, we're nice guys here at the Bureau. We're going to give you the same chance we gave him." Woodrow sat down opposite Harper. "Give us a statement, and we'll go easy on you." He put Martinelli's letter in his breast pocket.

"What does 'easy' mean, exactly?" Harper stared at the letter sticking out of Woodrow's shirt. He wondered what Martinelli had said. He'd probably blamed Harper for everything. Everyone always did.

"You know, Harper, cons don't like cops in prison. You'll be just another plaything to them. They'll eat you alive."

"How do I know that's really a confession? I know Jonah pretty good. I don't think he'd sign nothing." Harper sat back in the chair, seemingly in triumph.

"Are you some sort of raving idiot?" Woodrow flew to his feet, ripping the letter from his pocket angrily. "Look! Is this Jonah Martinelli's signature, or isn't it!" He unfolded the paper and pointed to Jonah's name.

Harper wanted to read the entire thing, but Woodrow's hands were covering the rest. For a split second, Harper thought about asking, but Woodrow looked like a wild animal hovering over him with a snarling grin.

"Y—yeah. It looks like Jonah's," Harper replied meekly.

Woodrow sat down. "Well, then, are you going to cooperate?"

Harper shook his head. "I don't know. I don't know if it would really be to my best interest."

"You ever been to prison before? It's not anything like Club Med. You know what happens when the lights go out?"

"All right. All right. What do you want to know?" Harper conceded.

"Good. Good," Woodrow said before going over to the door. "Okay," he said to someone Harper couldn't see.

Seconds later a video camera was wheeled in and set to roll. Then, Harper and Woodrow were left alone.

"First, Harper, I want you to tell the camera your name and that you are doing this of your own free will."

Harper complied.

"All right, how did you make our undercover agent—the man you knew as Rylan Andies?"

Harper looked directly into the camera, then fidgeted and looked at Woodrow.

"Look at the camera, please," Woodrow said, suddenly sounding very cordial.

"I saw this stranger sitting in a car. I thought his voice sounded familiar when I talked to him, but I couldn't place it. You know what I mean?"

Woodrow didn't answer.

"Anyhow," Harper continued, "I didn't really think much of it until I saw him with Ry. I don't know why. I just thought it was fishy, so I tailed them. Then I knew."

Chapter Eighteen

Nina and her father were returning home from enjoying a long walk when Lance's excited expression met them at the door.

"You'll never believe this," he said.

Lance ushered them through the door with the excitement of a child at Christmas. "Here. Sit. Sit."

They sat down and shared a smile over Lance's animated emotion.

"What is it, Lancelot?" Rich asked.

"Harper confessed!"

Rich sprang to his feet. "He confessed?"

"Confessed?" Nina echoed.

"He confessed to everything. All of it. Drugs in the tequila, in the toys—even woven into the fabric of T-shirts. It's amazing."

"How could he do that?" Nina looked amazed.

"The tequila bottles had an insert. The label covered the cocaine and the tequila covered the scent.

"But that wouldn't work," Nina interjected. "You'd be able to see it from the bottom.

"No," Rich cut in. "The bottles have nippled bottoms. You can't see in at all."

"That's right," Lance agreed. "As for the toys, it was in the hair mostly. He was a slick one, Carlucci was. He knew it would be too easy to detect stuff inside the dolls, so he wove the stuff into the hair and starched it into the clothing, just like with the T-shirts." He smiled and shook his head. "Harper told us everything! Even Margaret Orwell, that sweet mama-type at the B and B, she helped torch her own place. He said he had something on her—blackmail—wouldn't tell us what, though.

"Oh! I almost forgot." He reached inside his breast pocket and pulled out an envelope. "This is for you," he said to Nina, "from Jonah Martinelli."

"Let me have that!" Rich tried to grab the paper, but Nina pushed away his hand.

"Sorry," Nina said, eyeing Rich's surprised expression. "But it's for me."

"But . . ."

"No." She shook her head. "I want to read it." She took the letter and read it silently before noticing the anxious looks of Lance and Rich. "Okay, I'll read it to you," she said.

The letter read:

Nina Thomas,
I'm not a sentimental guy. I'm not real sorry for a lot of the bad things I've done, but I wanted you to know that I wouldn't have killed you. I wanted you to know that.
Jonah Martinelli

"That's a crock of bull," Rich bit out. "He's trying to cut a deal."

"I believe him," Nina told him quietly.

"You sure have a funny way of telling the good guys from the bad guys," her father replied.

She stood up. "Look, I can't explain it. I just believe him, that's all." She turned and left the room without giving Rich another chance to speak.

"But . . ." Rich tried to follow her.

Lance stopped him. "Let her go, man. She'll get over it."

The day was beautiful and sunny when Nina, Lance, and Rich got into the car. Nina was in high spirits—finally going to see Ry. She only hoped that no surprises would keep her from going to him this time.

She looked at Rich and smiled. Father. What a wonderful word. What a wonderful surprise. She'd only had him back for two days, but already it felt as though he had never left her.

She thought about her mother. Nina had picked up the phone several times to call her mother, but had decided against it each time. How could she tell her that her first husband wasn't dead. It would kill her. Nina had finally decided to wait until she got home and could tell her face to face.

As they entered Flagstaff Medical Center, reluctance rose in Nina's heart. It seemed a lifetime since she'd last seen Ry— and then she'd thought he was a gangster.

She fingered the tiny box that held the present she'd bought for him. She hoped he liked it.

She looked from Lance to Rich, one on either side of her.

"You okay? You look a little pale," her father said.

"I'm fine. Just nervous, I guess," Nina replied. "After all, I did mistrust him, didn't I? He might hate me, or something."

Lance answered. "He doesn't hate you, Nina. In fact, I'm willing to bet he likes you quite well." He smiled.

Rich's brow creased. "What's that supposed to mean?"

"Give it up, buddy," Lance told him. "She's too old for you to start being over-protective."

"Yeah, right!" Rich retorted as they reached the room. He opened the door for Nina to precede them.

She didn't expect Ry to be up and dressed, sitting in the chair, but he was.

"Hi," she said meekly.

"Hi. I'd get up, but I kind of wore myself out getting dressed," he told her.

She walked over to the bed and perched on it in front of Ry. "Why'd you get out of bed? Shouldn't you be resting?"

"I didn't think it would be fair for you to see me in my underwear since I've never seen you in yours."

The heat rose in Nina's cheeks. Rich cleared his throat and stepped farther into the room. "So, how you feeling today?"

"Pretty good. I'm glad to see you two together."

"Rich? Let's get some coffee for everyone, huh?" Lance still stood by the door.

Rich turned to face his friend. "Huh?" He glanced at Nina, then at Ry. "Oh . . . right . . . coffee. We'll be back in a jiffy."

Nina watched Lance and her father leave the room then turned back to Ry. "I'm sorry."

"For what? You don't have anything to be sorry about."

"Yes I do! I'm responsible for you getting shot. I should have trusted you." She threw her hands in the air and walked over to the window. She looked out at nothing in particular and then turned back to Ry.

He turned in the chair and looked at her. "You didn't get me shot. *I* got me shot. I did some really amateurish things back there. I shouldn't have had you at the house. I shouldn't have met Rich in broad daylight. It was dangerous and against procedure. I was a fool."

She turned and knelt at his side. "You're not a fool. You were concerned about me, and I really appreciate it."

"I told myself I was responsible for your safety since it was my father who had put your life in danger in the first place. But you know what? I've been lying in this hospital for a long time, and I've had a lot of time to think. I didn't do it to be responsible. I did it because I wanted to." He chuckled, but there wasn't much humor in it. "I'm supposed to be the big hero and save you, and I end up getting shot. How romantic is that?"

Nina looked into Ry's eyes and smiled. "It's romantic that you wanted to." Moments passed as their gazes locked in silent communication. She wanted to tell him how she felt about him, but she couldn't find the words.

Finally, she put the package she had brought into his hand. "Here," she said. "It's for taking such good care of me."

Ry grunted. "Good care of you? I almost got you killed."

"Just be quiet and open it," Nina told him.

He opened the tiny ring box and found two one hundred dollar bills folded into a small square. He looked at Nina and smiled. "What's this?"

"It's what I owe you, remember? You said you wanted cash."

He smiled and took it out of the box. Underneath it was a gold Saint Christopher medallion.

"My friend gave me one to keep me safe on my journey. I think it worked," Nina told him, bringing her hand up to cover the small necklace she wore hidden beneath her clothing. "That and lots of people looking out for me."

"I guess there's something you should know."

Nina raised her eyebrows.

"I'm Jewish."

Nina smiled. "That's okay. It will still work."

Ry chuckled. "Thanks. I'll keep it with me always." He gently kissed her cheek and then gazed directly into her face. Time seemed to stand still for a moment; then he spoke so softly that she almost didn't hear him. "I want to keep you with me always too." He touched his lips to hers, and she knew she would never have anything to fear ever again. She was home. With Ry. With her father. With her family.

She brought her hand up, touched it to Ry's face, and . . .

The door opened. "Hey, what's going on here?"

"Don't worry, Dad. I can take care of myself." Nina looked at Ry. "Right?"

"No, ma'am," Ry said, sounding official.

"What's that supposed to mean?" Nina grunted indignantly.

Ry chuckled. "That would be against procedure, ma'am. It's my job to take care of you now."

Nina's heart warmed. Her life new life with Ry was about to proceed.